THE HANDBOOK

DON'T MISS THESE OTHER JIM BENTON TITLES:

Victor Shmud, Total Expert #1:
Let's Do a Thing!

Victor Shmud, Total Expert #2:
Night of the Living Things

Franny K. Stein #1-7

Dear Dumb Diary Year One #1-12

Year Two #1-6

AND DON'T MISS ...

Dear Dumb Diary, Deluxe:
Dumbness Is a Dish Best Served Cold

THE HANDBOOK

FROM *NEW YORK TIMES* BESTSELLING AUTHOR

JIM BENTON

Scholastic Press / New York

Library of Congress Cataloging-in-Publication Data available

ISBN 978-0-545-94240-9

10 9 8 7 6 5 4 3 2 1   17 18 19 20 21

Printed in the U.S.A.   23
First edition, October 2017

Cover design by Jim Benton
Page design by Yaffa Jaskoll

For Griffin and Summer,
who would never try to manipulate me.

THE HANDBOOK

PROLOGUE

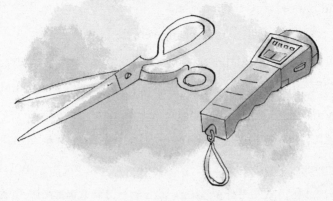

Agent Washington ran a hand through his thin brown hair as he drove slowly through a quiet neighborhood. None of the agents really appreciated getting "Cruise the Neighborhood" assignments, and Washington resented these most of all.

Washington picked up the microphone.

"I'm on Torry Street, a couple streets south of Banbury, halfway down the block," he grumbled. "Look, it's getting late, nothing is going on. Maybe we can just call it a night here and—"

Just then, a child's voice screamed from behind some hedges.

"Help! Help me!"

Washington didn't hesitate. He threw the car into park and barked into the handset.

"Child in distress. Exiting vehicle."

He followed the screams through a dense cluster of bushes until he found himself in a tiny clearing, surrounded on all sides by high shrubs.

"This would be a pretty good place for an ambush," he whispered to himself as he slowly reached for his immobilizer. He checked the battery indicator. He had a full charge.

Suddenly, small forms, dressed entirely in black, charged from all sides and crashed into him, driving him down hard on his stomach and sending his weapon flying.

One of the attackers stood on his neck while the others swarmed over him and worked rapidly to expertly tie his hands and feet behind him. A blindfold followed, then a gag.

He twisted and struggled to escape the ropes, but his attackers knew what they were doing.

"Shut up and lie still," the attacker hissed. It was the unmistakable voice of a young girl.

Washington's mind reeled. *These are kids,* he thought, and he heard another one of his assailants speak into a walkie-talkie.

"Marion here," she said. "Capture test a success. Enemy agent subdued. I have his weapon."

"Be careful with that," a boy's voice on the speaker cautioned her.

"I know," she snapped. "Don't talk to me like I'm an idiot."

"Of course you're not an idiot. Those immobilizers aren't lethal, but they will knock you out and they hurt like crazy. We all just want you to return to base unharmed."

She rolled her eyes and put the walkie-talkie in her pocket. She leaned in and inhaled Washington's scent deeply.

"He's a dad," she said.

"How can you tell?" one of the masked accomplices asked.

"I'm picking up coffee, shaving cream, and Fruit Roll-Ups. A man this age only has Fruit Roll-Ups if there are kids in the house."

The boy's voice crackled over the walkie-talkie.

"Marion. Release subject unharmed. I repeat, unharmed."

The girl calling herself Marion huffed.

"I'm not kidding, Marion," the boy said seriously. "*Unharmed.*"

She forced Washington to roll over, and laughed as she

pulled aside his blindfold. She wore a black bandana over most of her face, and he could see nothing of her features but her dark, angry eyes.

"My commanding officer says I shouldn't harm you. But don't you get tired of people telling you what to do, like all the time? Like they think you're stupid."

The other masked kids nodded and murmured in agreement.

Agent Washington swallowed hard.

"I sure do," he said nervously. "I can really relate, Marion."

She chuckled softly.

"How about when people that don't even know you use your first name in an attempt to make you think that you're friends; do you ever get tired of that?" she asked.

The kids fell silent. Washington realized that he had crossed a line with her.

The boy's voice came over the walkie-talkie once more.

"Give him the scissors, Marion," he ordered.

"Oh, I'll give him the scissors, all right," she said with a low chuckle.

She raised her arm and he tensed up, but she brought the scissors down hard in the dirt, just inches from the side of his head.

She exploded with laughter at his frightened expression and stood up.

"Let's go," she commanded her squad, and they vanished silently into the darkness, leaving Agent Washington to roll around helplessly in the grass for the next ten minutes. He managed to wriggle the dull scissors out of the ground and clumsily snip and saw through the tough ropes.

By the time he got back to his car, sweating, humiliated, and clutching at a broken rib, other agents were there, waiting with gigantic grins, to hear the story of how he had been ambushed and disarmed by a bunch of kids.

CHAPTER ONE

Trash Day.

It came every Friday on Banbury Road.

It's a truly wonderful day, a bit like Christmas, except the gift givers were not aware that they were giving anybody a gift, and it's not uncommon for the gift to be a dirty diaper.

Jack's next-door neighbors, the Wallaces, had just sold their house, and an immense mountain of their discarded junk sat on the curb and beckoned to Jack. It's not often that this much high-quality trash gets piled up on the curb, and it was calling to Jack like a big, filthy, discarded mermaid. Jack was helpless to resist it.

Jack's mom didn't understand the value of harvesting other people's trash.

How many times had Jack heard her lecture him end-lessly about the topic?

"Can you imagine what people will think of you? And you could cut your hand on something. Sometimes people throw away acid and things like that and you could be scarred for the rest of your life. Acid could dissolve off your face. Is that what you want, a dissolved-off face?" she would ask, her voice reminding Jack of a handful of spoons in a garbage disposal.

And seriously, was the answer to the question ever in doubt?

Why, yes, Mother, a dissolved-off face is the coolest new thing. It's exactly what I want.

But he couldn't think about her lectures just then. He needed his full trashful concentration.

Jack rode around the pile, circling it like a shark, like a shark analyzing his prey, like a blond, green-eyed shark throwing occasional glances over his shoulder to see if his mom was watching.

Mom knew how to move the drapes ever so slightly, just enough so that a single accusing eye could glare through the gap. Jack knew that if she did the Drape Gap Move at this very moment, she would see the trash acquisition in progress, throw open the front door, and start howling like a baboon with its tail caught in a lawn mower.

The mission would fail, the trash would not be acquired, and this was precisely why, he was certain, sharks never brought their moms along on hunts.

He knew she was probably busy washing clothes or washing dishes or washing a tree or any of the other million things that moms apparently love to wash, but she could be unpredictable at times and had disrupted his plans more than once. *Precision*, he thought. This was a mission of precision. He noticed that the phrase *mission of precision* kind of rhymed and he felt that this made it more legitimate somehow.

There were no flies buzzing around the pile. This was a good sign. Flies meant that there was a lot of icky garbagey stuff inside, like half a tuna casserole, or kitty litter, or the other half of that tuna casserole. Jack remarked to himself that if people really cared about kids, they would throw away only nice things.

Jack had picked through more than his fair share of trash in his young life, and he had come to realize that adults apply a kind of science to trash stacking.

Adults like to get hernias, which is some weird condition brought on by lifting something that you are not strong enough to lift. So the boxes they balance on the top of the pile are lightweight. This means that these boxes are either empty or have only a couple useless articles of holiday decorations, or worse: maybe Mrs. Wallace's old bras.

Jack briefly recalled an experience with a discarded old-lady bra that he had encountered as a much younger trash picker. He had pulled it slowly from the trash can and handled it curiously for a full minute before it occurred to him exactly what it was he was holding, and that it had been the very recent property of the million-year-old woman smiling and waving shyly from her porch. This is when he discovered that it is not possible to die from a case of the willies. If it was, Jack's short life would have ended right there.

Jack shook the bra memory from his mind and returned to his analysis of the boxes. The boxes at the bottom of the pile, the heavy ones, could contain things like toys, magazines, or power tools. Yes, it's the bottom boxes where one must direct one's attention. It's all about focus.

Unfortunately, while focusing his attention on the bottom boxes, Jack lost focus on things like potholes and gravity. That split second of carelessness sent him wobbling and clattering to the ground, a scraped-up tangle of bike and angry twelve-year-old.

Please oh please oh please, Jack thought to himself with his eyes scrunched shut. *PLEASE don't let Maggie have seen that.*

Maggie was the prettiest girl in the world, and the only girl whose opinion mattered to Jack. She had lived across the street for about two years, and he had worked very hard to conceal his dorknicity from her.

He wouldn't want to be seen acting like a dope in front of Maggie if she was merely the Most Mediumest-Looking Girl in the world, either. And if we're being honest here, even if Maggie was the goofiest-looking girl in the world, Jack would rather eat unsweetened oatmeal out of his math teacher's shoe than appear stupid to her.

Maggie was pretty, but way above that, she was smart, and Jack respected that. He opened his eyes slowly and looked with a cringe in the direction of her house.

She wasn't looking. Maggie hadn't seen.

His coolness remained intact.

Then he looked back over at his house. His mom wasn't running out in a panic with Band-Aids and antibiotics.

That meant she hadn't seen, either. Nobody had. The mission was still on.

He quickly grabbed a box of heavy trash from the bottom of the heap, balanced it on the seat of his bike, and walked it swiftly into his garage, its weight teetering and shifting on his bike the entire way.

He stashed it in the corner behind a plastic sled, a set of golf clubs, and a recycling bin that they weren't using as much as they should be.

Just as he had finished concealing his treasure, the door from the garage to the house flew open and Jack spun around to see his mom standing there, holding a large spoon in one hand and a bag of frozen vegetables in the other.

"What have you done to your pants?" she screeched. "And where's your helmet?"

He looked down. In his crash, he had torn the knee out of one pant leg.

"Do you have any idea how much pants cost, young man?" his mom shouted. "I'm sick and tired of you destroying all of your new clothes the minute you get them." She waggled the bag of frozen vegetables at him in what was probably supposed to be a threatening manner.

Jack tried to open his mouth to say something, but his

mom was well practiced at spotting a mouth opening and could start yelling again with the blinding speed of a whip cracking.

"And don't give me any smart-aleck answers either, young man. Your father and I work very hard to make sure that you and your sister have nice things and a roof over your heads."

For a moment, Jack's mind began to wander. Does anybody have a roof under his head? Would his parents prefer a dumb-aleck answer? Did his mom know how much she sounded like a goose when she was angry? What exactly is an "aleck" anyway?

He snapped out of his thoughts just in time to hear Mom wrap up the lecture. He was always glad that he had thoughts like those to occupy his mind while his mom was talking.

". . . And the next time you'll be grounded! Now wash your hands for dinner, and for the millionth time, turn off the garage light."

What did Mom really mean when she said "grounded"? Like, you'll be buried in it? Chained to it? Or was it like telling a pilot that they aren't allowed to fly?

News flash, Mom: I don't have a plane.

Jack walked to the bathroom to wash up, and stopped briefly by the front window. He squinted. Across the street, he could see his best friend, Mike, his black hair hanging down in front of his eyes, trudging past a window, followed by his angry dad, who was waving his hands furiously. Mike was getting yelled at, too.

"I wonder how many kids, at this very moment, are getting yelled at by their parents," Jack said to himself, and began doing some calculations on a slip of paper.

He looked at the figures and nodded.

"Yes," he said. "According to my math, it's exactly one buttload of kids."

CHAPTER TWO

Jack wiped his mouth and put his napkin on the table. He knew that he had committed the serious crime of Not Eating Everything on His Plate, and was pretty sure that Dad, who thought of himself as Chief of the Food Police, was going to make an arrest.

"Finish your dinner, pal," Dad said, looking at Jack over the top of his glasses.

"Dad, if those glasses are supposed to help you see, why do you look over the top of them all the time?" Jack asked.

"Just finish your dinner."

"Dad, I'm full."

Jack's little sister, Jessica, decided to be the Dinner Deputy and provide some backup to Officer Dad.

"Maybe he ate some candy or something," she offered, "and he soiled his appetite."

Jessica was perfectly adorable, from her sweet little pigtails to her pert little nose. She lisped the tiniest bit, due to a tooth that had recently fallen out, and that slight lisp was the thing that had pushed her over the edge from supercute to perfectly adorable. Her perfect adorableness, however, was not something her brother could appreciate.

"That's SPOILED, pinhead. Candy could SPOIL your appetite. Or cake could SPOIL your appetite. Or your sister's face could SPOIL your appetite," Jack said, and he sneered at her in such a way as to let his five-year-old sister know how dumb he thought she was, how dumb she had always been, and how dumb she would always be even if she went to college for a thousand years. True, that's an awful lot to get across in a single sneer, but Jack was good at sneers, and he had sneered this particular one many times before.

"There are people starving in India, and you leave your sister out of this," Mom snapped. She jabbed her fork in the air at him for emphasis.

Jack sputtered.

"Wait a second, Mom. *She's* the one that stuck her nose

into my business. And, by the way, why don't we FedEx our leftovers to India once in a while if you're so concerned about the starving people there. And hey—let's put Jessica in the box as well, and while we're at it . . ."

Dad's face got bright red, but not the jolly red of a lollipop or a balloon. It was more like the red of an itchy rash or a monkey butt. The sight of it made Jack freeze in mid-sentence. It was not the red that any face should ever be.

"Do you think that food grows on trees, young man?" he bellowed, bringing his fist down on the table like a meaty cannonball.

Jack knew he should have stayed quiet. Only an idiot would have responded to that particular question at that particular moment.

"Yeah, Dad. Lots of food grows on trees. It's called fruit. Ever hear of it?" he said smugly.

The next thing Jack knew, he was in his messy room, wondering why his parents were always asking if he thought something grew on trees. They also liked to ask him if he thought they were made of things, like when he asked them to buy him a phone: *Do you think I'm made of money?* they would ask. *Do you think I'm made of phones?*

Sometimes he would answer, but it often turned out that they didn't really want answers to those questions, which was confusing, because if he delayed for even a moment on other questions, they would sometimes impatiently shout, "ANSWER ME!"

It was times like those that Jack wondered if there was a psychologist that his parents were supposed to be talking to four times a day but that they never had talked to him even once and never would and they weren't taking the medicine he wanted them to, either.

Up in his room, Jack stepped carefully though the clutter on his floor. He looked like somebody crossing a creek full of clothing by stepping on randomly placed carpet stones.

He moved quietly toward his computer. The standard rule was that if he had been sent to his room, he was not allowed to get on his computer. But Jack figured he could be quick and quiet enough to log on, send Mike an email, and jump off before his dad had a clue.

Technically, it would be against the rules, but he was pretty sure that if you said *technically* before you said a rule, this meant you didn't have to follow the rule.

He tiptoed over to the desk and prepared to quietly type in his password. He gently pressed the first key.

DING-DONG! A bell rang out!

Jack tumbled backward in a panic. Ohmygosh. Busted! His dad had installed some sort of alarm on his computer!

DING-DONG!

No.

Wait.

Jack laughed at himself. That wasn't an alarm. It was just the doorbell. His mom answered it and he could hear his parents talking to the Wallaces from next door. They had dropped in to say good-bye for the very last time. They were retired now, and they were on their way to the airport. Like most retired old people, they were headed someplace warm, which Jack thought was strange, because when you want to keep something fresh longer, you put it in the refrigerator.

"Bye, Jack," they called up the stairs, and Jack poked his head around the corner to wave.

"Bye, Mr. and Mrs. Wallace," he said politely. "Have a good time in Florida."

Mrs. Wallace gave him a big wrinkly smile. It had been a long time since their only son had moved away, and she was very fond of Jack.

"If you ever want to come for a visit, you're always welcome," Mrs. Wallace said. "There are lots of those amusement parks close by."

"I'd like that," Jack said, thinking how much he wouldn't like that, and he waved good-bye.

He wondered for a moment why people wait until they're old to retire. It seemed like they should have their fun while they're young enough to enjoy it, and then go get jobs when they got so old they couldn't do anything fun anymore anyway. Adults had everything SO backward.

CHAPTER THREE

Sometimes summer days roll past like a thunderous roller coaster, clattering and shaking with screaming howls of laughter exploding from the wild-eyed riders.

And sometimes summer days roll past like a dirty, underinflated little beach ball, wobbling and wiggling, and then coming to a stop because somebody neglected to stuff the plastic nozzle up inside it.

This Monday had been more like the little beach ball type day, and it was starting to look like the nozzle wasn't even plugged at all and the sad little ball of a day was slowly deflating.

Jack and Mike spent most of the morning doing nothing more than sitting on Mike's front porch. They tried a couple times to go indoors to play video games, or go online, but their moms chased them back outside.

"It's such a beautiful day out. You shouldn't be inside on a day like this. Go out and get some fresh air," they said, as they would always say.

"There's air *inside* the house, too," Jack would always point out. "It's good enough to keep you people alive. Let us stay inside, too."

That never changed their minds.

The two boys sat on the porch and threw tiny pebbles down the sidewalk.

"I'm so glad that Old Man Wallace moved away," Mike said.

Jack nodded in thoughtless agreement.

"He was crazy, you know. Like totally crazy. Like one time when I rode my bike across his lawn and he turned the hose on me."

Jack laughed.

"One time? You rode across his lawn all the time. And even my dad has turned the hose on you for the exact same thing."

"It's not just that," Mike said, and he slid up closer to

Jack, his voice falling to a whisper. "One time, I saw him kill a man—with a shovel."

"You did not!" Jack yelled.

"You don't know that," Mike whispered in the scariest voice he could manage, wiggling his fingers for additional effect.

"I DO know that."

"Okay. Let's agree that neither one of us knows for sure if he killed a man or not," Mike whispered. "But the truth is that he kills them all the time. Probably."

Jack laughed and shoved him over, not an easy task to do: Mike was only a little taller than Jack, but thirty pounds heavier.

"Mike, you are so full of it I can't figure out why it doesn't squirt out your ears," Jack laughed.

The two of them traded stories about Mr. Wallace, like the one time they saw him dancing through the front window of his house, and another time when Mike made him so angry he starting yelling at him in this high, screamy voice that made him sound like a lady who'd caught rabies.

"What do you think he was like when he was our age?" Jack asked.

"I don't think he ever was our age," Mike said. "You know, a lot of old people never actually were young."

"That doesn't make any sense."

"No? Just think about it. What kid would have ever grown up and invented something like a necktie, or creamed spinach? Would a kid ever grow up and be all weird about how nice his lawn looked? No, my data shows that some people *must* have been born full-grown. It's the only explanation."

Jack considered the theory. It somehow made sense.

He looked over at his mom's minivan.

"You might be right, Mike," he said. "No kid would have ever said, 'One day, when I have enough money to buy any kind of car I want, I'm going to buy one that looks like a giant loaf of bread.'"

"My dad's car looks like a turd," Mike said. "I mean, why would you do that? He's seen all of the other cars ever made, and he still went with the one shaped like a turd."

By later that afternoon, they had run out of Mr. Wallace stories and had accepted the fact that Monday was going to be a boring day that would seem to last for weeks.

Jack had just found the right balancing point so that he could sit on his bike with the kickstand down and his feet up on the handlebars, when Maggie Dooley rode past on her lavender bike, which looked exactly like if you crossed a cupcake with a girl pony.

Maggie had a dusting of freckles across gloriously pink cheeks, and bright auburn hair that was always immaculately brushed, although when she rode her bike, most of it was hidden under her helmet.

Jack wanted to wave at her every time he saw her, but something always stopped him.

But things change.

Maybe it was the heat, or maybe it was because the day was moving so slowly, or maybe he was so completely overwhelmed by cheeks and lavenderness that he just couldn't help it.

For the first time ever, Jack waved at Maggie.

And then he looked away before he saw how she reacted.

"Mike," he whispered urgently. "What did she do?"

"She waved back."

"Was it like a *friend wave* or a *more-than-a-friend wave*?"

"What would a more-than-a-friend wave look like?" Mike asked.

"Like maybe she giggled a little or, like, waggled her

hair?" Jack said, flipping his head a bit to demonstrate what hair waggling might look like.

"Why didn't you watch for yourself?" Mike asked, annoyed. "What difference does it make anyway?"

For Jack, it made a *lot* of difference.

For him, Maggie had just changed his saggy-beach-ball day into a roller-coaster day. He didn't know why she had that effect on him, and Jack wondered if it was difficult for her to always be that pretty. He thought that maybe being that pretty all the time might actually hurt, like straining to lift a tremendous amount of weight, or hold in a fart. Not that he believed she did that—fart, that is—but if she did, it would probably sound pretty, like a jingle bell or flute. Maybe a harp. He also wondered how Maggie made him think about stupid creepy things like that, and he made himself stop, but not before concluding it was probably a flute.

CHAPTER FOUR

Maggie parked her bike in the garage and put her helmet carefully on the seat.

"Hi, Mom," she called out as she came in the side door.

Her mom was on the phone and took a break from the conversation only long enough to say, "Look at your hair. Do you want it to look like a bird's nest? Can't you do something with it?"

"It's from the bike helmet, Mom," she said. "The one you always tell me to wear. See, when I wear the helmet, then it makes a mess of m—"

Her mom had already turned her conversation back to her friend on the phone.

"Oh, her hair is just a tragedy. A catastrophe. All over the place. Like a haystack in a tornado."

Maggie hated being talked about that way, but protesting would only result in an argument. The easiest thing to do was to go and brush her hair.

She walked up the stairs to her room.

Maggie's room was lavender, but not *merely* the lavender of her bike. It was Super-Lavender. It was the lavender like the frosting that tiny fairy bakers use on the precious little cakes they give to itty-bitty girl pixies to congratulate them on how cute they are. Her room was exactly that color.

Not that Maggie chose the color. She didn't even like it. Her mom chose it for her, and bit by bit, more lavender stuff was added—lavender sheets, lavender drapes, lavender carpet, and a lavender lampshade. The color reflected off everything in such a way that anybody standing in her room looked as if they had a bad violet sunburn.

Maggie looked all over for her hairbrush and couldn't find it—until she glanced out the window and saw her little brother, seven-year-old Sean, doing something with it out in the backyard.

"Sean!" she yelled as she thundered down the stairs, scrambled out the door, and ran into the backyard.

"What are you doing with my brush?"

"I'm brushing the lawn," he explained.

She looked at his work. The three-foot-wide path of neatly brushed grass snaking around the backyard suggested that he had been doing it for quite some time.

Maggie yanked the brush from his hand.

"Look what you did to my brush," she yelled. It was filled with clumps of dirt and grass, and the bristles were stained bright green.

"But look how nice the lawn looks," Sean said, somewhat offended that Maggie failed to appreciate how hard he had been working.

She noticed several little grass ponytails and a little patch held in place with one of her barrettes.

"Okay, maybe the barrette didn't work out as good as I thought it would," Sean admitted.

Maggie stormed inside, slamming the door behind her.

"MOM!!" she yelled.

Her mom hung up the phone.

"Don't come in here screaming unless the house is burning down," she yelled back at Maggie. "Do you want the neighbors to think that we're a bunch of maniacs that the police have to come and take away? Is that what you want?"

"Look what Sean did to my brush," she said, waving the evidence angrily at her mother.

Sean burst in ready to defend himself.

"I was only brushing the lawn," he said.

Maggie's mom stood for a moment with her hands on her hips. Then she started giggling.

"Brushing the lawn!" she repeated. "Oh, Sean—you really crack me up." She gave him a big hug, looked at the brush, and started giggling again. She reached for the phone.

"I have to call Alice and tell her this one."

Maggie's mouth fell open. "You're not going to punish him? At least yell at him?"

Her mom glared at her.

"Maggie! He's a *little boy*. He doesn't know any better."

"He's only five years younger than I am. You would have yelled at me five years ago."

"Just go wash the grass out of it, Maggie. It'll be fine," her mom said, and started giggling again. "Brushing the lawn . . ."

Maggie began stomping out of the room.

"Hey, Maggie," Sean said.

She didn't feel like hearing an apology from him at that exact moment, but at least an apology was something.

"Don't forget your stupid barrette," he said, flipping it at her. He had carefully entwined a worm around it.

She made her nastiest face at him just in time for her mom to turn around and see.

"You want your face to freeze like that?" she snapped.

"Faces don't freeze!" Maggie shouted just before turning down the hallway.

"They do, too!" her mom yelled. "Kids make ugly expressions like that, and their faces freeze. Happens all the time! They have them lined up in the emergency room."

Maggie flopped down in her chair and threw the brush in the trash. She stared angrily at her computer screen.

"All the time, huh?" she grumbled, and she started searching online for examples of kids' faces freezing in ugly expressions.

And she ran search after search right up until dinnertime.

CHAPTER FIVE

"Because I said so, that's why," Mike's dad sighed.

"How is that a reason?" Mike protested. "I only want to do a little gaming before dinner."

Mike's dad had a lot of rules. He had rules about bedtime, even on days when Mike didn't have to get up early in the morning. He had rules about how much time Mike watched TV, even though he, himself, wasted hours and hours watching golf and the news and other things nobody cared about.

And the rules kept on coming, every day, like he was making them up as he went along. And to Mike, it seemed the only reason his dad could ever give him for the rules was this:

"Because I said so."

And Mike's response was always "How is that a reason?"

"Drop it, Mike," his dad said. "No video games right now. No TV either. Do something else. Read a book."

"Can I read a book about video games?" Mike asked, his face posed in a smug sort of *gotcha* expression.

"Sure," his dad said, replacing the look on Mike's face with one of pure disbelief.

"So you're saying that I can *read* about a video game but I can't play one?" he squawked.

"Of course."

"Dad, that makes no sense. First, you're against video games and then you're for them? How does that make sense?"

His dad was trying to watch the news, and Mike had taken a position directly between him and the TV. "Because I said so. Now move out of the way. And get your hair out of your eyes. It looks ridiculous like that."

Mike decided to take a stand, and he folded his arms defiantly, shook his head to make his bangs cascade even farther down his face, and remained standing directly in front of the TV.

His dad exploded from the chair and threw open a

cabinet next to the TV. He grabbed the game controllers and shook them at Mike.

"You want to act like a brat? You'll get these back when I think you're ready. Now go wash your hands for dinner."

Mike stormed into the bathroom and washed his hands sloppily.

"How is that fair?" he complained angrily. "All I wanted to do was play a few stinking minutes of video games!"

CHAPTER SIX

Jack stared at the fish sticks on his plate. He had only taken a little nibble of one, and he could feel his mom and dad staring at him as they slowly chewed their food.

Dad broke the silence. "Why do we have to go through this every single night at dinner? What's the problem, Jack?" he said.

"No problem," Jack said.

"Why aren't you eating your dinner?" his mom demanded.

"I don't like fish sticks," Jack said.

"Of course you do," she said. "You've been eating them since you were a baby."

"Then I guess I must have eaten all I'll ever need by now."

"Sit there until you finish them," his dad said.

Jessica smiled like a chimp at Jack. "Yeah, you sit there until you finish them," she repeated.

"You stay out of this," Dad barked.

"I love you, Daddy," she said.

It was a feeble attempt, but one that occasionally worked. Dad smiled at her and she smiled sweetly back. She then dutifully picked up her plate to carry it into the kitchen, and as she passed Jack, she grinned at him again, possibly even more chimp-like than before, and that image of her mocking, chimpy face lingered with Jack for quite a while.

Time passes slowly for a person staring at a plate of fish sticks, and Jack's mind began to wander: Why did they call these sticks? When they make them out of chicken, they call them "fingers." Why don't we serve other animals in finger form, especially the ones that actually have fingers? And most significantly of all, if parents *really* want you to eat your dinner, why don't they just serve food they know you like? How simple is that?

Jack pushed the fish sticks around on his plate. He smushed the canned peas into something that looked like green clay and stirred the mashed fish into it. He began to carefully swirl in the squooshed peach slices until his entire plate looked like something that might remain behind in an alien's egg after it hatched.

With the side of his fork, he began sliding it all into a mound in the center of his plate, which he built higher and higher into a magnificent little heap of pure yuck.

"You just about done?" his dad asked him, making Jack jump. He had been standing behind Jack, watching Mount Revolting take shape.

"No," Jack muttered. "I have about two more hours to go on this before it's perfect."

His dad sat down. "Look, Jack," he began, and his voice didn't sound all "daddish." He sounded more like one regular person talking to another regular person.

"I know fish sticks aren't your favorite. They're not my favorite, either," Dad said.

"Wait a second," Jack said, plunging his spoon straight up and down into his plate of gunk. "Are they Mom's favorite?"

"Nope. And your sister doesn't like them much either."

"Dad. Listen to yourself. They are NOBODY'S favorite. You and Mom are in charge. Why the hell wouldn't you have at least SOMEBODY'S favorite?"

Jack's mom walked in and picked up on Jack's loose use of the word *hell*. Then she got a good look at her dinner sculpted into a disgusting lump of smushed goo.

Dad tried to calm things down with a big, broad smile, but it just made his face look like something that somebody had hurriedly carved into a pumpkin.

"Jack! Go upstairs. That's it. That's it," she howled as she followed him to the staircase. "Go upstairs and stay in your room!"

Jack went to his room. He hated being sent off like that, but at least dinner was over—for him, anyway. He could hear his mom downstairs. This wasn't completely over for her.

"Perfectly good food, and look what he does to it! Honestly, what makes him do that? Well, nothing for him until morning. He can go to bed hungry!" She made sure that she yelled loud enough for Jack to hear.

Jack flipped through a magazine and looked out the window. He started to get hungry, but he knew that asking for something to eat would start up a big hairy fight.

He thought about playing his music really loud, mostly because he knew his parents hated that, like all old people do.

He lay there for a while, wondering why old people hate loud things. You would think that if your hearing was bad, you'd *want* everything loud.

It made no sense.

"One day, when you're old, there's a moment when you turn the music down and you never turn it back up again," he said to himself. "Do you know you're old when it happens? Are you aware of the exact moment?"

He fell asleep in his clothes with the lights on.

CHAPTER SEVEN

Jack dreamt about salami. He dreamt that a big fat salami sandwich showed up at their house in the middle of the night because it had lost something. The salami sandwich resembled his old neighbor, Mr. Wallace, and it was telling his dad over and over about needing to get this thing back.

And then Jack woke up, and he looked around his room.

Somebody had come in, pulled off his shoes, and left a salami sandwich for him on his bedside table. *Must have been Mom*, he thought. Every time she sent him to bed hungry, she brought him something to eat later.

His room was dark, except for the dim light from his clock radio. He looked at the time. It was 6:00 a.m. He took a bite from the sandwich and pulled off his socks.

He wasn't sure exactly what had awakened him so

ridiculously early. Jack was sure that if you looked outside this early, you'd see birds and squirrels asleep on the sidewalk.

And then he heard a voice like the big fat salami sandwich he'd dreamt about. It was coming from downstairs.

He walked quietly to the door and opened it just enough to slip through. He snuck down the stairs and peered around the corner. His dad, barely awake, was talking to Mr. Wallace.

"I thought Mr. Wallace moved to Florida," Jack whispered to himself.

Mr. Wallace was a mess. He was unshaved, his clothes were wrinkled, and he kept pulling his fingers through his messy white hair.

"It's just like I told you on the phone. I looked everywhere," he said. "I don't know what's going to happen."

Jack's dad patted him on the back.

"It's going to turn up," he told him in a reassuring voice. "You're not the first person in the world to have lost something, you know, but let's not talk about it on the phone again."

Jack's mom brought in a tray from the kitchen.

Mr. Wallace nodded knowingly.

"You're right," he said. "Never know who might be listening."

"Oh, nobody's listening," Jack's mom said with a

dismissive little laugh. "Let's sit down, have some coffee, and think about where it could be. I'm sure we'll have you back on a plane to Florida before you know it."

So Mr. Wallace HAD moved to Florida, Jack thought. But then he flew back here, in the middle of the night three days later, just because he lost something? What? What could be that valuable? He knew that Mike would tell him that it was probably a corpse.

Jack sat down on the step and listened carefully.

Mr. Wallace was rambling.

"We didn't take it to Florida. It's not in the old house or the garage. What if I never find it? What if I never get it back?"

Jack wanted to hear more, but it was still pretty early, and even when it wasn't early, most of the time when adults talked, he wanted to fall asleep. He figured he should head back up to bed.

As he got to the top of the stairs, he heard his dad say to Mr. Wallace, "The two of us should drive out to the dump and have a look."

THE DUMP! Jack suddenly felt recharged. Many times he had imagined what a dump would be like, and he pictured it being exactly like a Walmart full of aisles of great trash you can just take for free.

CHAPTER EIGHT

He pulled on his pants, stepped on half a salami sandwich, grabbed his shoes, and ran out the door, pausing only long enough to pick up the stomped sandwich and stick it in his mouth.

THUMP THUMP THUMP THUMP THUMP, he came rushing down the stairs.

"Dad? Dad?" he shouted.

"STOP SCREAMING!" his mom screamed. "YOUR SISTER IS STILL TRYING TO SLEEP!" she screamed with ever-increasing volume.

"Where's Dad?" Jack asked.

"He had an errand to do. Why?"

"I don't know. I just wanted to know. Never mind. I don't know. No reason."

Saying any more than that would have revealed that he had been listening in on their conversation. But it was exactly the kind of meaningless jabbering that alerted Mom to a *Lie in Progress*.

"No reason, huh?" she asked.

"No reason, Mom. I mean, I'm curious, okay? No reason for you to dump all this junk on me."

"*Dump* this *junk*, huh?"

How did she do that? Jack realized she was pulling it out of him like some sort of a Jedi, or worse, like some sort of Jedi's mom. That's probably where Jedis learn mind tricks, from their moms.

"Going over to Mike's house!" he shouted back to her, as he escaped through their front door before he revealed anything else.

He ran across the street, where Mike was in his driveway, tossing up clumsy shots at his basketball hoop in his pajamas.

"If I make this shot, you have to pay me a hundred dollars, okay?" he said, a single eye peering from behind his messy bangs.

"No. Listen, Mr. Wallace was at my house this morning and . . . Why are you out here in your pajamas?"

Mike missed the shot.

"I thought I could make that one," he said. "See? If you had bet me, you would have won a hundred dollars."

"It wasn't a bet," Jack said quickly. "And why are you out here in your pajamas?"

"The gravity of the sun messes up my shots, so I decided to come out and shoot a few before the sun showed up."

"The sun is still there," Jack said, "even when you can't see it. The gravity is still there."

"That explains why I missed that shot, I guess. Good point, Jack."

"But listen—Mr. Wallace lost something important. Something valuable."

Mike caught the ball.

"Valuable?"

"I think so," Jack said. "And my dad took him to the dump this morning to find it."

"So THAT'S the hobo I saw with your dad."

"Maybe it's a briefcase full of money," Jack said.

"Maybe it's a Pegasus," Mike suggested. "One of those flying horse things."

Jack paused, looked straight at Mike, and cocked his head like a dog does when it hears a peculiar noise.

"You think Mr. Wallace lost a flying horse? *That's* what you think? How would you lose something that big? And what makes you think there even is such a thing?"

"You said it was something valuable. What would be more valuable than that? Anyway, they have *wings*, stupid. It could have flown away. God, Jack, use your head," he said, slapping his forehead with his palm.

"So, you're saying that you *really* think it might have been a Pegasus?"

Mike tossed his bangs back and looked at Jack with both eyes; he felt vaguely insulted by Jack's tone. He knew how to put Jack in his place.

"Let's go ask Maggie if she hopes it's a briefcase full of money or a Pegasus," he said, and took off in a full run for Maggie's house.

"NOOOO!" Jack yelled, bolting after him and making the tackle before Mike had gotten more than fifteen feet.

Mike squealed in the highest, girliest voice he could, "I'm Maggie, and I weally weally hope it's a pwetty fwying pony, Jack, so we can get married and fwy away on a big dumb honeymoon of wuv."

Jack stood up and watched Mike roll around on the grass, howling with laughter. Kicking him always just made him laugh harder, so all Jack could do was wait for him to quiet down on his own.

They spent the rest of the morning arguing about what Mr. Wallace lost, with Mike threatening to go tell Maggie about the Pegasus every single time Jack made fun of his guesses.

After a few hours, Jack's dad's car came around the corner. Jack waved and motioned him to stop.

Jack's dad rolled down the window.

"What is it, Jack? I'm kind of in a hurry here."

"Where were you?" Jack asked.

"I, uh, had some stuff to do. We'll talk more later," he said, and pulled into their driveway. Jack watched him walk quickly into the house, brushing himself off as he went.

Mike ran across the street toward Jack's house, and Jack had no choice but to follow him. Mike ran into Jack's garage.

"Quick! Let's go in and see what they're talking about," Mike said, and the two of them slipped in quietly. They hid next to the doorway and listened carefully.

Jack's dad was flustered. He talked loudly as he described the morning to Jack's mom.

"First off, there's no dump, not like what I was imagining. I don't know what we were thinking. Our trash goes to a landfill and the closest one is an hour's drive from here. And there's no way to know if Wallace's trash is even above-ground anymore. They're constantly bulldozing stuff under."

"Did you look around?" Jack's mom asked.

"Well, yeah. Kind of, but you have no idea. A dump like this is a massive operation. You wouldn't even know where to start. And the people there won't let you wander around looking for stuff. There's big machinery and trucks every-where. You could get killed."

"Where's Mr. Wallace?"

"I dropped him off at his son's house. He's hoping that maybe his son picked it up last time he was in for a visit."

"Should we . . . report it?"

Jack and Mike looked at each other. "I have to pee," Mike whispered to Jack.

"Report it? And get us in trouble, too? There's no rea-son to report anything," Jack's dad said. "It's just *misplaced*, that's all."

Mike tugged on Jack's arm. His whisper was louder and more urgent. "Every time I hide, I have to pee. You know that."

"Well, if it doesn't turn up soon," Jack's mom said, "we could get in trouble anyway."

Jack whispered to Mike, "What could they get in trouble for? What is this about?"

Mike's eyes crossed. He couldn't hold it any longer. "We have initiated Launch Sequence," he whispered, and ran out the door, letting it close behind him with a loud slam.

Jack, thinking quickly, covered the sound of the door slam by pretending he was walking into the house. "Mom!" he yelled. "Do we have any German chocolate cake?"

"Cake?" his dad said. "Since when do we eat cake in the morning?"

Jack had the answer to that. He thought to himself: *We have coffee cake, hotcakes, pancakes. We have cake things for breakfast all the time.* But this wasn't the time to make Dad mad.

"Oh, right," he said, and made a quick exit.

Out the window, his parents watched him run across the street to Mike's house. "Look both ways, look both ways," his mom whispered through clenched teeth.

CHAPTER NINE

Mike and Jack sat on Jack's front lawn as the sun went down on a fairly unusual day. They were absentmindedly ripping handfuls of grass out of the lawn and waving off mosquitoes.

"Why do mosquitoes come out in the evening?" Jack said. "Wouldn't it make more sense to come out during the day when more people are out?"

"If I was a mosquito," Mike said, "I'd try to get all the other mosquitoes to help me steal a whole bottle of blood from the hospital and then we'd take that back to our mosquito house and drink it until it was gone."

Jack stared at his best friend. He felt that there was no doubt that Mike was a very special kind of stupid, but he couldn't really argue with him about the blood bottle. It actually was a pretty good idea, if mosquitoes could pull it off.

"If we put a raw steak out on the ground, would mosquitoes bite it?" Mike asked.

Before Jack could answer, Mike ran off toward his house.

"I'll see if we have one!" he yelled.

Jack lay down on the cool grass and looked up at the purples and yellows of the evening summer sky. He closed his eyes and started snickering at the idea of mosquitoes robbing hospitals.

"What's so funny?" Maggie said.

She was standing directly over him, looking down. He hadn't heard her walk up.

Jack scrambled to his feet. "Mosquitoes," he said, "stealing hospital blood."

Maggie smiled politely. Jack felt as though he had just been punched in the face by her prettiness.

Maggie sat down as Mike returned. They had no idea why Maggie had decided to join them, but it was okay with them. Jack and Mike looked at each other, shrugged, and sat down as well.

Must have been that wave, Jack thought. *I should have waved a long time ago. I must be a pretty good waver.*

Mike pulled a raw steak out of his pocket. "Look," he said, and tossed it on the grass.

Jack felt a little embarrassed and apologetic. "Mike's doing an experiment. He wants to know if mosquitoes will try to suck blood from a raw steak."

Maggie giggled. "Cool," she said.

"Do you think they will?" Mike asked her.

"I don't know. The meat might not be enough to make them bite. They're attracted to heat, and the carbon dioxide that animals exhale. Also, the juice in meat isn't blood, exactly. It's mostly water mixed with something called *myoglobin*. Most of the blood drains out during slaughter."

Jack slapped at a mosquito that was biting him.

"How do you know that?" Jack was visibly impressed with how smart she was.

"The web," she said. "I read a lot of stuff online."

"Do your parents let you go online whenever you want?" Mike said enviously. "My parents watch every little thing I do on the computer."

"Not whenever I want, but pretty often, I guess." She looked directly at Jack. "We should chat sometime."

Maggie's dad called to her from her front porch.

"Mags! Let's go!" he shouted.

"I gotta run," she said, and started toward her house. "He'll freak out if I don't hurry up."

"See ya," Mike said.

"Blug-buh," Jack said.

He had meant to say "bye-bye," but his throat was choked up with the new respect he had for her, which he was trying to swallow on top of the stomachful of pure crush he already had.

Maggie stopped and turned back to them.

"Oh, one more thing. Have either of you EVER heard of a kid whose face really and truly froze in an ugly expression they made?"

"Like his?" Jack said, pointing to Mike's face.

Mike pointed at his own face for clarity.

Maggie shook her head. "No, like this," she said, and twisted her face up into a spectacularly ugly expression.

They shook their heads no.

"I didn't think so," she said. And there was something about the way she said it that made her seem like a detective, which, on top of her appearance as Internet master, bug scientist, and world's prettiest face, made Jack feel like he might vomit Pure Total Crush out on the grass, which would probably be bad for the lawn and get him yelled at.

They watched her run up onto her porch and into her house.

"Maybe we should go to the dump," Mike said.

"Huh?" Jack said numbly, still thinking about Maggie and his crush vomit for her.

"Maybe your dad just isn't very good at trash picking. Maybe if you and I went, we could find whatever it is Mr. Wallace threw away. We're the best trash guys in the world. Remember that one time you found that totally awesome giant bra?"

Jack shivered. "Don't remind me," he said, and he looked up at Mr. Wallace's house, just in time to see a curtain flutter slightly.

"Did you see that?" he said. "Somebody is inside the Wallace house."

"Like a deformed hobo?" Mike said hopefully.

"I saw the curtain move. Somebody's in there."

"It's probably some sort of deformed hobo," Mike repeated. "Let's get my dad's golf clubs and attack him."

The debate over the rightness and wrongness of attacking a deformed hobo had to wait. Jack's mom called him to come in for the night, and Mike sat down on his own porch, knowing that he would be called in next.

"I think it would be cool to find a giant bra," he said.

CHAPTER TEN

Early the next morning, Maggie was awakened by the sounds of a loud police radio out front. She staggered from her bed and pushed back her hair so she could see. From her window, she saw three police cars across the street.

She ran downstairs and out the front door.

Her mom, dad, and brother, Sean, were on the lawn, watching the small crowd of neighbors and police standing on the sidewalk outside the Wallaces' old house.

She spotted Jack and Mike in the crowd and waved.

Jack trotted over to her happily as Mike trailed behind.

"Hey, Maggie," Jack said.

"What happened?" she said.

Jack began to answer but Mike interjected.

"Got your basic deformed hobo incident," Mike said, hiking up his pants with authority.

"No. No deformed hobos. Somebody broke into the Wallace house. I heard one of the police say that the place had been torn up pretty bad, like some walls ripped down and stuff," Jack said.

"Yeah, your deformed hobos *will* do that. And the mutated hobos, too," Mike added. "If science has taught us anything, it's that a mutant hobo has the strength of ten gorillas."

"Did they catch anybody?" Maggie's mom asked. Her voice sounded concerned.

"I don't know. They've been inside for a while. Maybe they caught somebody."

"I bet that hobo was looking for whatever it was that Mr. Wallace lost," Mike said.

Maggie's dad turned to Mike. He suddenly looked very serious.

"Wallace lost something?"

"Yeah. He lost something and he came back all the way from Florida to find it."

Maggie's mom laughed. "What could be so important that . . ."

She caught her husband's eye. He wasn't laughing.

There was a tension Jack didn't understand, and all of his instincts told him to get the subject changed.

"Nice pj's, Maggie," he said.

It suddenly occurred to Maggie that she was standing there on her front lawn, in front of Jack and Mike, wearing her adorable tiny lavender short pajamas. Her face turned bright pink.

"You know," Mike offered with a thin smile, "Jack sleeps in the nuuuuude."

He bounced his eyebrows up and down.

Maggie's little brother, Sean, began to howl hysterically.

Maggie's mom pursed her lips in a tight, small frown.

"Yes, well, that's all very nice. Inside, Maggie," her mom said, quickly shuffling the family back into the house.

As the door closed behind them, Jack shoved Mike hard.

"In the nuuuude? What was that about?"

"It was one of my famous conversation killers. We both knew that conversation was going somewhere bad. You, my friend, only know how to change subjects. I *destroy* them. That's why people call me El Destroyo."

"Nobody calls you that."

"You *should* call me that. People would think you were a

lot cooler if you were friends with somebody named El Destroyo."

As they walked back to his house, Jack looked over his shoulder at Maggie's. Mr. Dooley was standing at the window, watching the police at the Wallace house.

"Maggie's dad seem a little weird to you?"

"All dads seem a little weird to me, Jack. Every single one of 'em. Every time it snows, my dad runs outside to shovel it."

"What's weird about that?"

"After it rains, he doesn't run outside with a mop."

Maggie started up the stairs to her room.

"Maggie," her dad began. He sounded concerned. "Come back down here. That thing that Mr. Wallace lost; do you know what Mike was talking about?"

"No idea."

"You know it's important for you to tell us if you hear about anything . . . strange."

"Strange?"

"You know, if you see something or hear something that seems *unusual*. You'd tell us, right?"

Maggie thought for a moment. "There is one thing."

Her dad's eyes widened.

"Mike put a steak on the lawn to see if a mosquito would bite it."

Her dad's face went blank. Her mom smiled a little.

"I don't think mosquitoes will bite something dead, but if you think about it, it would be pretty smart if they did, because that way, they wouldn't get swatted."

Maggie's dad tried to smile, but there was deep concern hiding beneath it.

"That's it? Nothing about Mr. Wallace?"

Maggie's mom interrupted. "That's a pretty strange thing to do with a steak, all right," she said. "Now go upstairs, Maggie, and do something with your hair."

Maggie walked up the stairs. She paused and waited quietly for a moment, hoping to overhear something.

As she went into her room she heard her mom say, "She doesn't know anything. The other two don't know anything. Stop worrying."

Maggie's dad agreed.

"I'll try," he said.

Across the street, just behind the police cars, Agent

Washington spoke quietly into his phone, discreetly making careful notes about everything and everyone he noticed.

A little farther down the street, astride a bike, talking on her phone, was someone he didn't notice at all.

"This is Marion. I'm checking on the intercepted message."

CHAPTER ELEVEN

By lunchtime, Mike and Jack had been chased out of Jack's house twice. They had been chased out of Mike's house once. They had come to the point in a lazy summer day where they were inventing things to do.

The first game of the afternoon was to stand on a basketball and see how far they could roll it up Mike's driveway. Mike had seen bears do something like this in a circus act and he insisted that it must not be that difficult.

One second into his attempt, Mike fell off and went down hard on his back. This made his mom pop out their front door like the bird in a cuckoo clock.

"You want to break your back?" she yelled. "And be in a wheelchair the rest of your life? Stop standing on the basketball!"

Then they went over to Jack's house and started sword fighting with sticks.

Jack's mom yelled out the window. "You're going to put an eye out with those. Stop it! You want to get an eye put out?"

Mike and Jack dropped the sticks.

"She always says that," Jack said. "It's always 'you'll put an eye out.' If sticks were really that dangerous, wouldn't bank robbers use them?"

Mike laughed. "Yeah, they'd be all like, 'I've got a stick and I'm not afraid to make your vision, like, half as good!'"

"Yeah, and then the police would rush in with their automatic sticks that could put out twenty eyes per second."

"Yeah, and like, 'Two people were injured in a drive-by eye-putting-out today. Police have a suspect in custody and are doing tests on the stick to see if it is, indeed, the putting-out weapon.'"

The boys laughed for a long time and Jack grabbed the basketball from Mike. He set it down on his driveway and balanced on it for a mere second before his mom popped out the front door.

"You want to break your back?" she yelled. "You'll be in a wheelchair for the rest of your life! Stop standing on the basketball!"

He hopped off. Mike and Jack stared at each other, both somewhat puzzled.

"Did she just say the *exact* same thing my mom just said?" Mike asked slowly.

"Pretty darn close," Jack said. "How weird is that?"

"I told ya—don't get me started on moms. If Mom had her way, she would toss out everything that I could hurt myself with. And that's a *lot* of things."

He stared seriously at Jack.

"I've accidentally hurt myself a lot."

Jack looked blankly at Mike. He could feel a thought assembling in his mind.

"Like even pizza. Remember that time I hurt myself with a pizza? Who could hurt themselves with a pizza?"

Jack nodded. "It was a frozen pizza and you tried to use it for a bike wheel," he responded absently.

"Yeah, but—"

Jack interrupted him.

"Hang on. You said that your mom would *throw all the stuff away*."

"Yeah, and—"

It suddenly occurred to Jack. He paused on every word, giving each its own special emphasis.

"Threw. It. Away."

"Yeah, okay," Mike said. "Threw it away."

"I just remembered. I took a box from the Wallaces' trash and hid it in my gara—"

Mike instantly sprinted across the street and fumbled with the handle on Jack's garage door before Jack could even finish the sentence and scramble to his feet. It always amazed Jack that, for a chubby guy, Mike could move pretty quick when he wanted to.

"Where? Where is it? Where is it?" Mike shouted. He was already in the garage rooting around.

"Be quiet," Jack said. "You want my mom to come out?" He moved the plastic sled, the golf clubs, the broken pogo stick, and the recycling bin out of the way, and dragged out a cardboard box.

"Close the garage door," he said. "Let's take a look at what we have here."

CHAPTER TWELVE

"This is it," Mike said. "We'll always remember this as the moment we became millionaires."

"What do you mean *we*? I'm the one that grabbed the box."

"Look, unless I tell on you *right this second*, I'm an accomplice in this. That means that I'll wind up taking half the blame, so I'm entitled to half the money."

"I don't know," Jack said.

"I understand," Mike said calmly. "I understand perfectly. Well, see ya later. I have to go tell on you now. Hey, Mrs. Hartfield?"

He began walking to the door, watching Jack's reaction over his shoulder.

"Okay. Okay. Sit down. You can have half."

Mike smiled. "I really don't like sticking a loaded mom in somebody's face, you know. But you left me no choice."

"Whatever. Just . . . just help me figure out what we have here," Jack whispered.

"Okay, but if you find any game controllers in there, they're automatically mine," Mike added. "Since I'm the game master and everybody calls me THE GAME MASTER."

"I thought you said that everybody called you El Destroyo."

"I am known by many names, child."

Jack shook his head and slowly opened the box. Their faces, lit only by a couple garage lightbulbs, were frozen in joyful expressions of greedy delight as Jack extracted the first priceless treasure.

It was an old electric drill.

Mike grabbed it from his hand. "It's a rare antique drill!" he said, and he ran over and plugged it into a wall socket. He smiled broadly, pulled the trigger, and got an enormous crackling shock that knocked him backward onto his butt.

The lights in the garage flickered and Jack helped Mike to his feet.

"Th-that wasn't the treasure," Mike said, and he walked slowly back over to the box, wiping some drool off his chin.

Mike reached in and pulled out a book titled *Favorite Turnip Recipes of the World*.

"Turnips? Gross," he said. "This sure ain't the treasure either."

Jack pulled out a broken picture frame, two coat hangers, a doorknob, and a handful of nuts and bolts.

Mike pulled out a pair of pliers that were rusted shut, a crusty paintbrush, and what looked like a wheel from a tricycle.

Jack looked at all the stuff. He looked at each individual item from different angles.

"Maybe we have to assemble these things somehow. Maybe these parts fit together or something."

Mike sat down and tried putting things together.

"Yeah. Like maybe it's some sort of doomsday device. Like to destroy the world," he said hopefully.

Jack joined him. They crammed the paintbrush into the spokes of the tricycle wheel. They bent the coat hangers around the doorknob. They balanced the picture frame on the pliers.

After a while, Mike stood up and shook his head in disgust.

"This is junk. Pure junk. This isn't what they were looking for," Mike said. "I'm going to go check on my mosquito steak experiment."

Mike and Jack loaded the miscellaneous stuff back in the box and slid it behind the sled, the clubs, and all the other clutter.

"You're right," Jack said. "I'll have to keep it all hidden until I can put it out next trash day. I don't want to get busted for garbage picking."

"It's almost dinnertime," Mike said. "I'll see you later."

Jack watched Mike walk down the driveway and cross the street. Mike stopped for a moment to miss a shot with his basketball before he went into his house.

Jack closed the garage and opened the door to the house. He looked back to see if he had remembered to turn off the light and noticed that he hadn't put the turnip recipe book back in the trash.

"No use digging the box out to put this one book back," he said to himself as he grabbed it and took it inside with him.

He plodded slowly up the stairs, still trying to figure out what Mr. Wallace was after.

He walked into his bedroom, tossed the book on the floor, and walked back down for dinner.

Fifteen minutes later, Jack found himself staring at the casserole on his plate. He had only taken a little nibble of it, and he could feel his mom and dad staring at him as they slowly chewed their food.

Dad broke the silence. "Why do we have to go through this every single night at dinner? What's the problem, Jack?" he said.

"No problem," Jack said.

"Why aren't you eating your dinner?" his mom asked.

"I don't like casserole," Jack said.

"Of course you do," she said. "You've been eating it since you were a baby."

"Then I guess I must have eaten all I'll ever need."

His mom and dad looked at each other and sighed deeply.

"I know, I know," Jack said. "I can just sit right here until I finish it, right?"

CHAPTER THIRTEEN

"Jack, Jack, wake up," Jack's mom said softly as she sat on the edge of his bed and shook him gently.

"Mmghblrg. Glur bluh," Jack grumbled.

"Jack," his father said. "C'mon, wake up, buddy."

"Blurf. Pudding. Flurb," Jack mumbled, still very much asleep.

"WAKE UP!" Mr. Wallace shouted, and Jack's eyes popped wide open.

"Mr. Wallace? What are you doing here?"

"Jack, listen to me," Mr. Wallace said anxiously. "Did you happen to grab anything we had out on the curb? You know, any stuff we threw out?"

"What time is it?" Jack asked, his voice still dry and hoarse.

"It's morning, son," Jack's dad said. "Get up. We need your help."

Jack slowly sat up on the edge of the bed. He looked at Mr. Wallace, who had never looked worse; his shirt was torn and sweaty, his hair was a dirty mess, and he was covered in dust and dirt.

"What happened to you, Mr. Wallace?"

Mr. Wallace stammered, "I, uh, was doing some household repairs. Just a little dusty."

"In your old house? Is that why the police came?"

"Yes, but it was a misunderstanding. Back to the point, Jack. I threw away some stuff when we moved. I set it out on the curb, almost a week ago. You didn't take any of that stuff, did you, Jack?"

Jack's mom interrupted. "Jack's not allowed to trash pick, so I know for a fact that he didn't get into anything you had piled out on the cur—"

"Yeah," Jack said. "I took a box of junk."

Jack's mom put her hand over her eyes and shook her head gently.

"But I didn't think you wanted it. It was out in the trash. I didn't mean to take anything important . . ."

Mr. Wallace smiled hopefully. "Of course, Jack. Of

course. I know you would never take anything you shouldn't. You're not in any trouble. But I lost something, and I think I might have thrown it out. Where is this box of junk now?"

"It's in the garage. I'll show you."

Mr. Wallace thumped him happily on the back. "Good man, Jack. Good man. There might even be a reward in this for you."

The four of them walked out to the garage, and Jack's dad opened the door for extra light. Across the street, Mike was in his driveway, missing free throws as always. Mike saw the garage door open and began walking over, dribbling his basketball as loudly as he could.

Jack's little sister, Jessica, wandered into the garage and buried her face in Jack's mom's leg, grumpily rubbing the sleep from her eyes.

Jack pushed the sled, recycling bin, and other clutter out of the way and dragged out the cardboard box he had taken from the Wallaces' trash. Mr. Wallace impatiently nudged in next to Jack and started digging through the contents.

Mike stopped dribbling the ball. He walked in and stood next to Jack.

Mr. Wallace pulled everything out. He dumped the box

over, every last nut and bolt clattering on the hard cement floor. He pawed through it all.

"It's not here," he said.

He looked behind the sled and tore the lid off the recycling bin. He spun around, scanning the entire garage.

"It's not here," he said, the panic in his voice rising. "It's not here. Was this everything you found, Jack? You didn't find anything else? Like a book?"

"A book? What does it look like?"

"It looks like two cats sucking a lemon, Einstein," Mr. Wallace snapped angrily. "It's a *book*, Jack. What do you think it looks like?"

Mike blurted out an answer before Jack had a chance to respond.

"Nope. No book. That was all of it," Mike said. "Nothing else."

Jack and Mike were *very* good at conveying messages to each other with nothing more than a subtle glance. They could communicate everything from *I think it is very funny that you are getting yelled at right now* to *Somebody has made a bad odor and I believe it might be you.*

But with the particular glance that Mike was shooting

at Jack that very moment, he was saying *We are lying about the book. Stay with me on this.*

Jack understood the message.

Mr. Wallace eyed Mike with suspicion. He knew that whenever a foul word was written in the street with chalk, or noise was being made too early on a Sunday morning, or when something weird, like a steak, turned up in your front yard, it was usually Mike who was responsible.

"How do *you* know what was in the box, Mike?" he asked suspiciously.

"Jack always shows me what he trash picks. We went through it last night. Your old drill electrocuted me. But I probably won't sue you for it. Although I could, what with me being a child victimized by the carelessness of an old wrinkly adult and everything. A lot of juries would assume you did it on purpose, since most attempted murderers are all shriveled and wrinkly, no offense."

While Mike spoke, Jack's dad was considering the old drill being discussed for his own workbench. He held it up by the cord.

"So this is no good?" he said to Mr. Wallace, who shook his head no. Jack's dad unhappily tossed the old drill back in the box.

Mr. Wallace stooped down to talk face-to-face with Jessica.

"Jessica, honey, did you notice Jack carrying around an old book?"

Jessica smiled.

"Did you, sweetheart? Did you see Jack with a book?"

Jessica grinned. "I don't think Jack can read," she giggled.

"At least I'm not afraid of the zombie that lives in the basement," Jack countered.

"There is no zombie in the basement," Jessica shot back.

"OH MY GOSH!" Mike shouted, looking as terrified as possible. "THE ZOMBIE GOT OUT OF THE BASEMENT! EVERYBODY! RUN!"

"Stop it!" Jessica said nervously.

"BUT DON'T HIDE IN JESSICA'S ROOM BECAUSE I'M PRETTY SURE IT'S HIDING UNDER HER BED!"

"You boys go play now," Jack's mom said, shooing them away as if they were flies. They ran across the street and started shooting hoops in Mike's driveway.

Mike grinned proudly.

"Another conversation destroyed by the Great El Destroyo."

Jack laughed. There was no denying that Mike was good at destroying things.

"So why did you want us to lie about the book, anyway?" Jack whispered.

"You tell me," Mike said. "Why did you take the thing?"

"I was just too lazy to put it back in the box."

"Maybe there's something folded up in between the pages, like a hundred-dollar bill," Mike said.

"A hundred-dollar bill?" Jack said, amazed. "You think he'd fly back from Florida in the middle of the night and go through all this for a hundred dollars? You really have no idea how much things are worth, do you?"

Mike shrugged and tossed the basketball aimlessly at the net.

"So, if it's not a hundred, go get it and let's see what the big deal is."

"I will," Jack said, and turned toward his house. Across the street in his driveway, he saw his mom, dad, and Mr. Wallace talking quietly and looking at them.

"Hi, Maggie," his mom called out, waving in their direction.

Maggie? Jack thought as he turned and saw that Maggie had quietly walked up and was standing beside him.

"How do you do that?" Jack blurted out, surprised.

"Do what?"

"Move so quietly," Jack said.

"Girls are quieter," Mike said. "Scientific fact."

Maggie thought for a moment and nodded in agreement.

"But if girls are quieter, then how come *moms* are louder?" Jack said.

It was a fair question and Maggie scrunched up her nose as she puzzled on it.

"Because, stupid," Mike said, "moms aren't girls."

"Well, they're not *boys*," Jack scoffed, and the three of them stood there, lost in thought, not saying anything. This was an interesting mystery and they scowled a bit as they silently contemplated it.

"Maybe they change," Maggie said, "when they become adults and get married."

"No way," Mike said. "My sister, Jen, is an adult and married, and she's supercool. She used to babysit us sometimes and once she let us try and see how many cans of root beer we could drink for lunch. It's five, by the way, if you're wondering. Five each. Six will kill you."

Jack nodded and laughed.

"Yeah, and one time she let us set up a lemonade stand out front with beer. Mr. Wallace called the police."

"She let you sell beer?" Maggie said.

"No," Jack said. "That's only what it said on our sign. Really, it was lemonade. But you should have seen how long the line was when the police showed up."

Mike's expression suddenly changed.

"But then she got married and moved out."

Jack knew how bad Mike missed his sister and he tried to console him.

"Jen didn't move far. You still see her."

Mike threw up another lousy shot at the basket. "Yeah. But hardly ever."

"Wait a second," Maggie said. "So she wasn't an adult and married when she let you do all that stuff?"

"So you think that maybe it's *marriage* that does it?" Jack asked as he looked across the street at his house.

Mr. Wallace and his dad were walking inside. His mom and sister were standing in the front yard with expressions of confusion and revulsion as they poked Mike's steak experiment with a stick.

With an accusation already forming on her lips, Jack's mom shot a look across the street at them, but nothing remained of the three but a gently bouncing basketball. They had anticipated her reaction and, with practiced agility, swiftly aligned themselves behind a single tree so she couldn't see them from her angle. It was the type of reflex that dealing with Jack's mom had taught them, and Maggie, swiftly pulled into the maneuver, giggled with admiration at its brilliance.

After a moment, Jack peeked from around the tree. "I think she went in," he whispered. "They're all inside now."

"I have to pee," Mike said.

"I know. Every time we hide," Jack said quietly.

Mike peered cautiously around the tree trunk.

"Okay. They all went inside. The coast is clear," he announced.

Jack said, "I hope they're not looking for the book."

"What book?" Maggie asked.

Mike and Jack looked at each other. They were asking themselves the same question: Should they bring Maggie into this?

Mike respected her non-girlish reaction to insect blood suckery, and her Internet expertness. Jack admired all that as well and had, in a very short time, come to think of her not only as The Prettiest Girl in the World but as a person he liked being friends with, even though she was of the girl species.

The boys nodded at each other simultaneously.

"It has a hundred-dollar bill in it," Mike confided.

Jack screwed up his face at Mike.

"That's not true. We don't know *what's* so special about it. But Mr. Wallace really wants it back. They're in there right now, probably looking for it."

"You hid it, right?" Mike said worriedly.

"I didn't exactly hide it," he said.

CHAPTER FOURTEEN

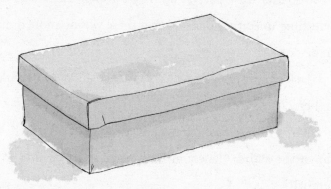

The three of them stood at the doorway to Jack's room.

"There are underpants on the lampshade," Mr. Wallace said in disbelief, as he surveyed the disaster that was Jack's room. "Why would you put underpants there?"

Jack's mom snatched them and put them behind her, feeling that the mess was somehow a reflection on her.

"What is that on the pillowcase? Is that salami?" Jack's dad said, his voice a combination of curiosity and disgust.

"Believe it or not, he cleaned this up yesterday," his mom said.

Sometimes when his room was messy, Jack's mom would say that it looked like a hurricane had hit it. Today it looked as though maybe the hurricane came back and brought a few of his hurricane buddies with him, and they took turns hitting the room. Then they invited their cousins, the tornadoes, over for a party, and they all spent the entire night wrestling until they decided that there was no more damage to be done.

Jack's mom turned to Mr. Wallace. "Do you think it's in here?"

Mr. Wallace turned away in disgust and walked back down the stairs. "It would have been easier to find in the landfill."

Jack's dad patted him on the back.

"We're not going to report this, Wallace. There's no reason to."

Mr. Wallace smiled. He was tired, but he was relieved at the kind words.

"It's probably buried under tons of filth by now."

Jack's mom jumped to Jack's defense.

"I would hardly call that tons of filth, Mr. Wallace," she snapped.

"I meant at the landfill," he said, and she exhaled a small laugh.

Jack's dad grabbed his car keys.

"Can I give you a lift to the airport?" he offered.

Mr. Wallace smiled and looked down at his own grisly appearance.

"Yikes," Jack's dad said. "Why don't you freshen up a little first? I'm sure I have some clothes you can borrow."

Mr. Wallace nodded in agreement.

Later on, from Mike's driveway, the three kids watched as Jack's dad and Mr. Wallace got into the car and drove off.

"I don't think they found it," Jack said. "Did you see how sad Mr. Wallace looked?"

"I don't speak Oldpersonface," Mike said. "They mostly always look sad to me. Or angry. I can never tell when they're happy."

"That's because you never make them happy," Jack said.

"So," Maggie said, her eyes filled with curiosity, "don't you think you should go in there and get that book? We need to have a look at it."

"My mom's still in there. How am I supposed to do that?"

Maggie thought for a second. "No problem," she said. "I have a plan."

* * *

Jack ran inside the house, slamming the door behind him loudly.

"Hi, Mom!" he yelled, waiting only long enough for her to come around the corner and see him.

He began bounding up the stairs to his room with a shoe box under his arm.

"Wait a second, mister. What's in the box?" she called up to him. Like all moms, she was very suspicious of things that come into the house in a box under a boy's arm at high speed.

From up in his room, Jack called down to her, "It's a box full of earthworms. Hundreds of 'em. I'm going to raise them in my room for pets."

Jack surveyed the tragedy that was his bedroom.

"I probably tossed it right about here," he said to himself as he dug down through the underpants, socks, and comics on his bedroom floor.

Finally, he hit the turnip recipe book in just about the place he had predicted.

His mom screamed up the stairs, "Earthworms?? You take those nasty things outside *this very minute*, young man."

Jack smiled. He took the lid off the box. There were no earthworms inside it, of course. It was empty.

"Oh, c'mon, Mom. Worms are so cool. Please?" He placed the turnip recipe book inside the empty box.

"NOW!" she screamed. "GET THAT OUT OF THE HOUSE!"

Jack moped down the stairs, carrying the box in both hands.

"Please?" he said quietly.

She opened the door and motioned with her angry mom head. She hated earthworms and Jack knew it. She watched him cross the street slowly and show the box to Mike. They both shook their heads sadly and went into Mike's garage, a brilliant bit of acting.

Inside, Maggie smiled and clapped her hands.

"That was a great idea, Maggie," Jack said. "It worked just like you said. I went in, put the turnip book in the box, and waited for my mom to tell me to get it out of the house."

Mike nodded with approval. "You're sneaky, Maggie. Are all girls this sneaky?"

Maggie grinned and rolled her eyes innocently.

Jack opened the box and the three of them looked at the book. It was an unappealing green color and looked old. It was the kind of book that could sit on a shelf for a thousand years, and nobody would ever consider picking it up.

Maggie lifted it out of the box and read the title.

"*Favorite Turnip Recipes of the World*?" she said, feeling a bit as though maybe she had been pranked.

"I know, right?" Jack said.

Mike grabbed the book and thumbed through the pages, shaking it up and down, waiting for the money to fall out.

"Nothing," he complained.

"You're *sure* this book is important?" Maggie asked, and the doubting look on her face stung Jack like a bee. Like an unbelievably pretty bee.

"Let's have a look," he said hopefully. "I mean, maybe old people would pay a lot for turnip recipes. Old people like turnips, right?"

"Turnips don't even like turnips," Mike said.

Jack started flipping through the pages. "Listen—I bet these are delicious, you know, for old people."

"What do turnips grow on, like trees or something?" Mike said.

"Turnips grow in the dirt. People dig them up," Maggie said.

"And then they eat them anyway?" Mike roared. "Old people have really questionable judgment, ya know? I mean, if somebody buries something in the dirt, there's probably a reason they buried it. Don't eat it, old people. Just leave it there."

Maggie laughed, but Jack had hardly heard anything Mike had said. Jack was reading.

"Guys," he said, "how weird is this?"

He opened the book's cover, revealing a second cover hidden behind it. This was *not* a copy of *Favorite Turnip Recipes of the World*.

Maggie examined the second cover and read the title aloud. "*Secret Parent's Handbook*?" she said. "What the heck is that?"

CHAPTER FIFTEEN

Maggie flipped through the pages, stopping on a random entry to read aloud. "Listen to this," she said.

The child may not always want to eat what you have served it. Use these methods, in any order:

1. Tell the child that there are people starving in India, or China, or any place the child has never been. It's important that they have never been there so that they cannot question the accuracy of the statement.

2. Tell the child to eat it so that it can grow big and strong. The child may desire this deeply, believing that once big and strong enough, it can defeat you.

3. Tell the child it will not receive a dessert if it does not obey.

4. Tell the child it must remain at the table until it has finished its dinner. You may also threaten to withhold other things the child desires, such as its playthings. THIS CAN BE RISKY as some children are stubborn enough to remain at the table all night.

5. Spank the child.

Mike howled. "I like how they call the kid an *it*. Oh, man, that's funny!"

Maggie handed the book to Jack. He flipped to the index.

"Let's see what it says about sticks," Jack said, and he flipped to a page near the middle. "Here we go.

> **The Strategy on Sticks: If the child begins to play with sticks, or anything long like a stick, warn it that it will get its eye poked out. Of course *you* know that eyes are very small targets and very difficult to hit, and the probability is much higher that the child will simply get lashed and receive a welt, but the image of an eye being gouged out is more frightening, and thus this is a better way to scare the child into stopping the activity.**

"It's like what our moms always say!" Mike roared. "Poke your eye out! Poke your eye out."

Maggie and Jack weren't laughing, and Mike suddenly felt uncomfortable laughing alone.

"It's funny, right?" he asked. "Isn't it?"

"See if it has something about faces freezing," Maggie said, and Jack flipped to a new entry and read it out loud.

> **The Face-Making Strategy:** If the child forms a repulsive expression on its face, tell it that it may freeze that way. Never tell the child that it will freeze like this *every single time,* or the child will know that you simply lied.

Maggie looked stunned. Then she looked angry.

"All those things. My parents have said all of those things to me. Those jerks," she said.

"I know, right? My parents, too. Jack, your mom and dad are always saying that junk," Mike said.

"I don't think we should tell anybody about this book," she said seriously.

"You don't think this is, like, a real thing that the Wallaces used, do you?" Jack said. "It's a joke book or something like that."

"It's probably a joke," Maggie said, flipping to the first few pages in the book. "But look, it doesn't have an author's name, or any dates, or any of the stuff you normally see in a book. And why does it have a fake cover? It doesn't even say who published it. Let me poke around online and see what I can find out about it."

"Your parents *were* acting pretty weird about it," Mike reminded Jack.

Jack handed her the box and she slid the book inside. "Okay," he said.

"Turnips," Mike chuckled. "Old people eat stuff they find in dirt."

CHAPTER SIXTEEN

Maggie slipped into her house. She smiled to herself. Mike was right: *Girls are quieter.* She slid silently up the stairs and into her room, and hid the box under her bed. Mission accomplished. She knew that later on that night she'd be able to secretly read more of it.

"What's in the box?" Sean asked.

Maggie jumped and whirled around. *Girls are quiet,* she thought, *but little brothers are phenomenal snoopers.*

"Underpants," she said without hesitating. "My girl underpants. Want to see them? They're very frilly. I think you'd love them." She began to reach for the box. "Try them on."

"Noooooooo!" Sean yelled as he ran from her room and down the stairs.

"Little brothers are great snoops, but they can be manipulated," she said, knowing that the book was safe from Sean's prying eyes for at least the next fifty years.

She sat down in front of her computer and started to search. And search. And search.

She found parent handbooks of every possible kind, with titles like *How to Raise Your Blond Left-Handed Teen* and *How to Raise Your Allergy-Free Child Who Wishes He Had an Allergy*, and the very popular *Adorable, Yes. But Is Your Toddler Adorable Enough?*

But she couldn't find any matches for the book Jack had found in the Wallaces' trash.

She looked for books of turnip recipes and found none, although, to her horror, she found millions of recipes for turnips and realized that there certainly are enough of them to collect in a book.

Before she knew it, hours had passed and her mom was calling her to come down for dinner. She plodded down the stairs, tired and frustrated.

Sean was already at the table, guzzling down his milk so fast that he was on the verge of drowning in it.

"Sean! You'll spoil your appetite!" Maggie's mom

scolded, and began setting out plates of hamburger-something-in-noodles-something with something-sauce.

"Ewww," Sean began to protest, before Maggie cut him off in mid-complaint:

"There-are-starving-people-in-China-you-need-this-to-grow-up-big-and-strong-if-you-don't-eat-it-you-won't-get-dessert-or-be-allowed-to-use-your-playthings-or-will-get-spanked," she said in a single breath.

Her mom and dad looked at her speechlessly. Then they looked at each other. Her dad narrowed his eyes. He looked skeptical.

"Where did *that* come from?" he asked.

Maggie felt a tension. That wasn't just a simple question. She was being interrogated. She knew the feeling. Her parents' voices took on a different tone when they were trying to get to The Bottom of Something. And this was that tone.

She smiled.

"That's what you guys always tell us, right?" she said, and began eating. "Mmm. Good," she added, hoping the compliment would push Mom off balance. It did.

"It *is* good, isn't it?" Mom beamed. "You know, I added

a can of blah blah soup to the hamburger and added in a little blah blah blah blah blah blah . . ."

Maggie didn't hear anything she said. She was thinking about how her parents had reacted when she had quoted the *Secret Parent's Handbook*. Did they know the book? Had they read it?

After dinner, Maggie and Sean argued about what to watch on TV.

"You always get to watch what you want," Maggie shouted.

"I haven't gotten to pick in a million years!" Sean yelled back.

"You don't even know how long that is."

"I do, too. There were dinosaurs a million years ago," Sean said confidently to Maggie, while casting an uneasy look toward Dad for some verification.

Their dad shook his head. "No dinosaurs," he said. "Most people say they went extinct sixty-five million years ago."

"Were there cavemen?" Sean asked.

"Yeah, I think so," Dad said.

"Was there Grandma?" Sean asked.

"You're such an imbecile," Maggie said unpleasantly.

"At least I'm not all in love with Jack, the nude sleeper, like you are," Sean said, adding, "and you're fat," just in case the stuff about Jack wasn't annoying enough.

Maggie blushed. She wasn't in love with Jack. She knew that love could take a person DAYS to fall into. But the subject was still embarrassing and she didn't feel like fighting anymore.

"Watch whatever stupid show you want. I'm going up to my room to read," she said, and she stomped up the stairs.

Once inside her room, she quietly closed her bedroom door and grabbed the box from underneath her bed. She began to read an entry titled "Broken Necks."

The child most likely has never seen a person with a broken neck, and the term "broken neck" might imply to the child that its head will fall off and is, therefore, effective in frightening it.

Perhaps the child is engaged in some sort of risky behavior. Ask it, "Do you want to fall and break your neck?" The fact that you have asked a question suggests to the child that it has a choice in the matter and is not merely being told to stop. Telling the child to stop doing anything can result in an argument, and so asking this question, however ridiculous it is, is a better way to confuse and frighten it.

Avoid ever asking the child any questions about a medical condition it has actually seen. For instance, if the child has met somebody that has broken his or her neck, change your example to broken back, or something of that nature.

Maggie thought the writing sounded old-fashioned. "When was this written?" she whispered.

She kept reading. The book had all sorts of suggestions:

If the child asks for something expensive, reply, "Do you think money grows on trees?" That way you will have saved yourself from the unpleasantness of

> **saying NO and will have inflicted on the child a confusing question that will temporarily distract it from thinking about the object it has requested.**

With every page, Maggie became more and more convinced that her parents had read this book. They might have even memorized it.

"Jack is going to want this book back," she whispered. "But I'm keeping a copy for myself."

She sat down at her computer and turned on her scanner. She riffled the pages. It was a long book.

"This is going to take a while," she said, and began a long night of scanning.

CHAPTER SEVENTEEN

"**S**it up straight," Maggie's mom said.

Maggie sat up. She had been up late and was looking a bit wilted. She stared at the unappealing bowl of cold cereal in front of her.

"And finish your breakfast. You know, it's the most impor—"

Maggie cut her off. "Important meal of the day? You're right. I wonder how that makes lunch and dinner feel. They're trying their best, too, you know—they try to be important, but there's breakfast, always the most important. Mom, don't you feel a little sorry for lunch?"

"*She feels sorry for lunch,*" Mom repeated, and laughed. "You're funny in the morning, Mags. I have to call Alice and tell her this one."

Maggie smiled. She had remembered a segment in the book:

> **The Breakfast Strategy: If the child will not eat its breakfast, tell it that breakfast is the most important meal of the day, as if to suggest that it has been proclaimed to be King of Meals. Children are not often persuaded by the fact that something is merely "important," but they often can be compelled by anything that is the *Most Important*. If the child argues, punish the child until it does as instructed.**

She knew that if her mom had read this *Secret Parent's Handbook*, she would have punished her for not eating breakfast, like a reflex. But since Maggie had reacted with something totally *unexpected*, her mom just dropped the subject and watched Maggie dump the cereal in the garbage disposal.

Sean got up from the table and prepared to dump his out, when their mom stopped him.

"What do you think you're doing, young man?" she said.

"I don't want mine, either," he said, and weakly pointed at Maggie's bowl.

"It's the most important meal of the day," she said. "You sit down and eat it."

"But I don't like it and you let Maggie—"

She cut him off before he could go on. "You eat that breakfast, young man, or no TV for you tonight," she yelled.

Sean sat down resentfully and started eating the soggy cornflakes. He listened as his mom picked up the phone and called her friend Alice to tell her Maggie's funny observation about feeling sorry for lunch.

A confused young Sean chewed slowly as Maggie walked past him, smirking triumphantly.

She kissed her mom and walked outside.

Maggie carried the book in a backpack swinging freely in her hand. Mike was already out in his driveway, busily missing basketball shots.

"Hey, Maggie, if I make this shot, you owe me forty dollars, okay?"

He looked at her backpack and pulled his hair from across his eyes. He looked around quickly to make sure nobody was listening in on them.

"Is that the book in there?" he asked, turning down the volume of his voice. He looked away from her as he spoke because he had seen spies do. that in movies.

"Yup," she said, and smiled. "I used it this morning to keep my mom from freaking out over breakfast."

Maggie recalled the earlier events to Mike.

"So, just by knowing the strategy she was using, you knew what to do to destroy it?"

"Yup. She depends on the rules so much, I don't think she has a plan B."

"Does that book have anything about video games?" Mike asked hopefully. "My dad is really strict about video games."

"Probably. It seems like it has something about everything."

Mike rolled the basketball onto the front lawn, and the two of them sat down in his driveway and read from the book.

There were entries on grounding, handwashing, kissing your grandma, and spinach.

After a while, they stopped reading, looked at each other, and laughed.

"It's amazing," Mike said.

"It's totally amazing, right? Because it's like you can almost hear your parents saying these exact things."

"No, I meant it's amazing that I read for a whole ten minutes and didn't fall asleep," Mike said. "Are all books this good?"

Maggie laughed.

Mike looked at her with no expression. He meant it.

"Oh," she said. "That was a real question. Well, there are lots of different kinds of books, Mike, and you would probably like some books and not like oth—"

"Hey, here comes Jack," he interrupted, jumping to his feet and grabbing his basketball. "Jack, if I make this shot, you owe me forty bucks, okay?"

Jack shook his head no.

Mike threw up a shot and missed.

"I thought I could make that. Well, too bad for you, Jack. I was going to give you forty bucks if I missed, but you didn't take the deal."

Maggie handed Jack the book, and as he took it, he concealed it under his arm.

"Maybe we should keep this thing hidden," he said. "Wallace is pretty hot to get it back."

"I think I understand why," she said. "Mike and I even found some stuff that could help him get his video games back."

"Now, *that* would be something. Mike's dad hates video games," Jack said, and ducked without looking as Mike missed another shot.

Maggie was impressed. "Good reflexes," she said.

"Yeah, well. You'll get them, too, hanging around with us," he said, and then he gulped hard as he suddenly realized he had issued something like an invitation.

"Not that—you know," he stammered. "Not that, you know, you were planning on hanging around with us because you probably have a lot of girl things to do like, uh, moisturize, or, you know, whatever. Your makeup and stuff."

"Moisturize?" Maggie said.

"I don't know," Jack began, and started to redden. "Like conditioners you put in your hair and lotion stuff."

Maggie laughed hard and punched him in the shoulder. "Not all girls are doing as much moisturizing as you might think, Jack."

Mike continued to take shots and miss. "*Moisturize.*" Mike giggled at the sound of the word as he repeated it.

Maggie pointed her finger at him and said forcefully, "And *of course* I'm hanging around. We have this book to figure out."

Jack smiled. He rubbed where she had punched his shoulder. It was hard enough to hurt, but he kind of enjoyed it. *Maggie's punches are like hot sauce*, he thought.

"I went over that whole book last night from beginning to end. It has a chapter on everything: mittens, flossing, crushes."

"Crushes?" Jack said.

"Oh. Y–yes," Maggie stammered. "Yes. I mean, and mittens. Flossing, too, was in there. With the crushes. Stuff like mittens. And the, um, crush stuff. Also vaccinations, I think."

She swallowed hard and turned as red as Jack had a moment ago.

The two laughed nervously. They had not noticed that Mike had been standing there watching their entire exchange. He looked slightly sick to his stomach.

"Does the book have anything about vomiting on your driveway because your friends are getting all cutesy-wootsy with each other?" he asked.

Maggie pretended to look at something in a tree as Jack started flipping through the pages. "Uh, let me check if vomiting is in here . . ."

Mike chuckled. "Forget that. You know what you should look for, Jack. See what it says about cleaning your room."

Mike turned to Maggie. "Jack's room is like if hogs fought a hog war in there and they used, like, underpants and socks for weapons."

Jack blushed. "It's not *that* bad, Maggie."

"Not that bad?" Mike roared. "I'm a slob. I mean it. I am a total slob. Really. And when I go into Jack's room, I'm, like, offended, you know? His room is so messy it actually *hurts my feelings*, like the whole room talked it over and decided to make me feel sad."

Jack loudly interrupted him.

"I found a huge section on room cleaning. This is going to come in handy. My mom has been on me for a while to clean it."

The three of them went into Mike's garage and took turns reading. Jack shared one entry that somebody had underlined with a pen.

Regarding Selfishness: The child is, without question, the most selfish creature in your home, and possibly, in the world. Know that it will always avoid work, responsibility, sharing, and hygiene. You must be fully prepared to respond to these disagreeable qualities, as it will display them constantly.

"Well, that's kind of insulting," Mike laughed.

"Yeah, but you see? That's *all* that they're prepared for. They're not ready for everything," Maggie said. "They don't know what to do when you don't act according to the book."

The three continued reading and sharing entries, and the longer they read, the stranger the book became. They read right up until they heard their parents calling them in for dinner.

CHAPTER EIGHTEEN

Mike studied his dad carefully. He was sitting as he always did after dinner, in his chair, watching the news, and this was *precisely* the wrong time to try to ask to play a video game.

"Hey, Dad," he said. "Can I switch off the news so you and I can play a video game?"

"What?" his dad said. "No. I'm watching the news here, Mike."

Mike opened his mouth to start complaining, but thought carefully about the *Handbook* and secretly glanced at a piece of paper with notes Jack and Maggie had given him.

"And if you think you're going to waltz in here and—" his dad continued.

"Oh, right. Sorry," Mike said, and slowly started walking out of the room and around the corner.

"I knew that wouldn't work," he said, wadding up the notes and jamming them in his pocket. "And who *waltzes*?"

Mike's dad sat for a moment and thought.

"Hey, Mike," his dad called to him. "Come here for a sec."

Mike walked back into the room.

His dad had a faint smile on his face. "Did you say *you and I* could play a video game?"

"Yeah. But you're watching the news. I'll go do something else."

"Hang on. Yeah, okay, the two of us. We can play. You'll teach me, right?" his dad asked, and he smiled broadly at his son.

Mike turned and secretly uncrumpled his cheat sheet to read one final note.

"Sure, Dad, but you'll probably beat me."

At that moment, across the street, Jack carried in his plate from the dinner table and set it on the counter next to where his mom and dad were rinsing off the dishes in the sink.

"Don't go running outside, Jack," his mom said. "Remember I told you I wanted you to clean your room today, and you didn't pick up a single thing."

"That's where I'm heading right now," he said, and he made sure to sound pleasant.

His mom blinked a couple times. The pleasantness had thrown her, just as they had predicted it would. "Yeah, well. You just see to it that you do, young man," she said. Her voice sounded a bit angry, but only because she had anticipated an argument and had gotten herself worked up in advance.

"Could you please hand me a garbage bag?" Jack asked. "Seriously, it looks like a hurricane hit up there."

She numbly handed him the bag. He could tell that she suspected something. It was time to employ the strategy that the three of them had worked up.

"I mean, how do you and Dad manage to keep *your* bedroom so neat all the time?" he asked. "There are *two* of you messing it up."

Jessica swiveled her head around. "Yeah. That's right. How do you guys do that?"

"Well," Jack's mom began. "It's probably because *one* of us works very hard to keep it nice and neat."

Jack's dad smiled awkwardly. This was the critical moment of the strategy, and Jack and Maggie had predicted two possible outcomes here: The first possibility would be that Jack's mom and dad would argue and then maybe forget about Jack cleaning his room altogether.

But that's not how it went. It went the way of the second outcome they had predicted:

Jack's dad said, "She does a great job, too. Doesn't she, kids? Jack, let's you and I go up and clean your room together. I probably need to do a little more of the cleaning around here anyway."

And he grabbed the bag and quickly dragged Jack up to his room.

They got up to his room and Jack's dad sat down on the bed. He handed Jack the bag.

"Here you go, buddy. Get to it. Clean this disaster up."

Jack knew that the whole strategy could have unwound here, but he stuck to his plan.

"Okay, Dad," he said. "Thanks for the help. I know this means you're missing the game."

It was summertime, and Jack knew that somewhere somebody was playing baseball on TV and that missing a game would make his dad nuts.

"Yeah," his dad said. "The game. I'm missing the game."

He grabbed the trash bag from Jack and began swiftly stuffing trash into it. He got faster and faster, tidying up this and straightening out that. He grabbed mighty arm-loads of laundry, running all the way down to the basement, starting the load, and sprinting back with paper towels and spray cleaner.

He changed the sheets on Jack's bed, then dusted, arranged, and organized so hard that Jack very nearly thought about helping him.

It had taken him no more than twenty minutes to accomplish what would have taken Jack six hours. Jack's room looked almost as if it had never been lived in. His dad sat on the edge of the bed to catch his breath at the precise moment his mom came around the corner and peeked in.

"OH MY GOSH," she said. "This is really amazing, Jack. Great job!" and she hugged him. She cast a glance over at his dad still sitting on the bed.

"Looks like your dad didn't lift a finger to help you," she grumbled. "Figures."

"No, Mom," he said. "Dad did most of this."

"Ha! Right," she scoffed. "You can go outside for a while. Stay out front where you can hear us when we call," she said. And Jack was down the stairs and out the door before she could change her mind.

Maggie was outside playing catch with her brother.

"Did it work?" she asked.

"Did what work?" Sean asked.

"Yeah. It was pretty amazing," Jack said, ignoring Sean.

"What was amazing?" Sean demanded.

"How do you think Mike's doing?" Maggie asked, also ignoring Sean, who was beginning to squirm with frustration.

"What is Mike doing?!" Sean yelled, prompting his mother to stick her head out the door.

"Sean! Be quiet! Why are you yelling? Maggie, why is he yelling?"

"I think Sean went in his pants," she said. "Want me to change him?"

"Sean!" Maggie's mom scolded. "Get in here!"

Jack and Maggie walked down to Mike's house, barely hearing Sean's screaming protests behind them. They stopped in front of the front window and watched Mike and his dad playing a video game inside. The two of them were laughing and jumping around, and the sight made Jack and Maggie giggle.

"Looks like it worked," Jack said. "What about you? How did you do?"

"I'm testing it tomorrow morning," she said, and the

two of them could hear her mom yelling at Sean from inside her house, two doors down. "Wish me luck."

The next morning, Maggie rolled out of bed and looked in the mirror. Every morning when she woke up, her hair was a spectacular swirling nest of auburn chaos. Most mornings, it would not be hard to imagine that a strong wind had blown bats into her room during the night, which, becoming entangled in her hair, spent hours and hours trying frantically to free themselves.

This morning was no exception, but just to make sure, she shook her head violently and made certain that it was the worst it had ever been. It was the only way to really test their strategies to defeat the book.

She looked at the old photo she held in her hand, and glanced over a page of notes she had made.

"Stop the fight before it starts," she whispered to herself, and walked down the stairs.

As she came around the corner, she saw her mom's mouth drop open, ready to go off on her about her hair. But Maggie was prepared and got off the first shot.

"Is this you in this picture?" Maggie said with a big smile. "You look like a model."

Her mom's mouth clamped shut with a soft popping sound.

"I love how your hair is so untamed and free. You look like some sort of carefree young socialite out on her family's yacht."

Her mom grinned and looked at the photograph. "That's from when your dad and I first met. I was hardly a model, Mags."

"Were you out on a yacht? Is that the ocean in the background?"

"That's old Skunk Pond," she said tenderly, her eyes filled with memories of youthful romance. "They drained it years ago after all those dogs got malaria," she said, still smiling sweetly.

She tilted her head and touched her fingertips to her lips gently. She looked like she was a million miles away.

"I want to look just like you did, Mom," Maggie said. "I love that young, breezy, young, carefree, young look you have here. I love how your hair goes where it likes and does what it wants. That's some young-looking hair you have there, Mom."

Maggie's mom looked at her and beamed. She hugged her close and laughed.

"Carefree hair, huh?" she said, and Maggie held her breath for a second, afraid that her mom had seen through the strategy. "Yeah, okay," she said. "We'll have to run a brush through this a *couple* times, but I know what you mean, Mags. You want it *breezy*."

And after a very short and very lighthearted hair-brushing session, Maggie's mom turned her loose, with her hair less fussed-over than she could ever remember.

She smiled, stuck her tongue out at Sean, and strolled out into the warm summer morning. Jack and Mike were already standing in Mike's driveway and she strode happily to meet them.

The three of them looked at one another and laughed hysterically.

"The book," Maggie said. "*It's real.*"

CHAPTER NINETEEN

Sometimes summer days roll past like a thunderous roller coaster, clattering and shaking with screaming howls of laughter exploding from the wild-eyed riders.

And sometimes summer days roll past like a dirty, underinflated little beach ball, wobbling and wiggling and then coming to a stop on its plastic nozzle, which somebody neglected to stuff up inside it.

And some days—some very special days—are like that roller coaster, but now you *own* the roller coaster, and you own the amusement park, and everybody in the park works for you.

The week had been one of those days after another. They had studied the book carefully, even memorized parts of it, and had discovered that by knowing what the book recommended to the parents, they could construct counter-strategies that would permit them to do almost anything they wanted.

Maggie was brushing her hair only when she felt like it and watching whatever she wanted on TV. Mike was playing video games for hours at a time, and sometimes playing with firecrackers in the driveway until very late at night. Jack had his mom helping him when he went trash picking, and nobody was on him to clean his room.

Outside of what the book said, their parents really seemed to have no actual ideas about how to handle kids, and that was just fine.

At times, Jack felt he had control over them that was almost hypnotic.

"More pizza?" Jack said, sliding the box across the table to Mike. Jack had arranged to have Maggie and Mike over for dinner, and had manipulated his parents into ordering pizza again.

"Sure," Mike said, and added a big scoop of ice cream to his plate as well.

"Sprinkles, Mike?" Jack's mom asked, and handed the bowl to Mike.

"Yes, please. And the gummy worms, too," he said, wiping his hands on his dirty shirt.

Maggie brushed her messy hair out of her eyes and grinned at Jack.

"After dinner we have dessert," Jack's dad said, and Jack smiled proudly, as if he was showing off some wild animals that he had trained to do impressive tricks.

"But isn't the ice cream already dessert?" Jessica asked. "We're having dessert for dinner."

Jack scowled at her. Who knew what kind of damage a statement like that could do to the progress he had made?

"Maybe you're right, Jessica. Maybe *you* should have vegetables for dessert," Jack hissed angrily.

Jack's parents looked at each other and looked at the ice cream. It was as if they were beginning to swim up out of a hypnotic trance, or shaking off the effects of a powerful mind-numbing medicine.

"Is this really . . . *dessert for dinner*?" his dad asked slowly.

"Ice cream comes from milk, and it would be pretty darned hard to imagine anything as high in calcium as milk," Maggie stated sternly. "So important for strong teeth and bones. And vitamin D has been linked to strengthening the immune system. Not to mention the antioxidants in the chocolate. You had better listen to me, Jessica; you sit there and you eat that ice cream or there will be no dessert for you."

Jack's parents looked at Maggie, then they looked at each other. Jack and Mike braced themselves. Maggie had gone too far: She had quoted the book's chapter on milk almost word for word, and Mike flashed a freaked-out look of astonishment at her.

But Jack's parents smiled and relaxed. They were so content that the correct words about milk had been spoken that they seemed to forget Jessica's remark about eating dessert for dinner.

"How many kids do you have, Maggie?" Jack's mom asked casually.

Maggie choked on her ice cream.

"Mom. Maggie doesn't have any kids!" Jack said. "She's my age."

His mom looked confused for a moment. "Oh. Yes. Of course. Where did I get that idea? I suppose because you know so much about milk and things. Silly of me," she said, laughing off her mistake.

After dinner they all went out into the front yard to eat Popsicles for dessert. Even Jack's dad, who didn't really like

Popsicles that much, had one after Mike explained to him about the kids at the equator who never get to enjoy Popsicles because they melt so fast there.

Then Jack and his mom started to have a pretend sword fight with sticks.

Everything was as it should be. The kids were calling the shots, the parents were easy to control, and life was a ball.

Jack's mom giggled like a little girl as she swished and slashed, but an unexpected slip on a decaying steak caused her to lunge forward awkwardly, and she drove the stick hard into Jack's face.

"Oh my God, I poked his eye out!" she screamed.

CHAPTER TWENTY

The nurse at the walk-in clinic put a little Band-Aid under Jack's eye. "That was a close one," she said. "An inch higher and you could have had your eye poked out. What were you doing, sword fighting with one of your friends?"

"With my mom," Jack said as he climbed off the examination table. "It was an accident."

The nurse turned and glared unpleasantly at Jack's mom and dad.

"You were sword fighting? With sticks?" she asked. "You know what could happen if you swing sticks around?" she demanded.

They nodded.

The nurse looked down at Jessica. "You okay, honey?" she asked sweetly.

Jessica smiled and said yes. The nurse picked up a jar of lollipops and offered them to Jack and Jessica. Jack took one but Jessica passed.

"No, thanks," Jessica said, and the nurse put the jar back on the counter.

"Don't like lollipops, huh?" she said as she finished filling out Jack's paperwork. She handed the form to Jack's mom as they began filing out of the examination room ahead of Jessica and Jack.

"I like lollipops," Jessica said. "But we had ice cream for dinner and Popsicles for dessert. I just don't want any candy right now."

Jack quickly added, "Our, uh, freezer broke, and you know, you can't let food go to waste," he said. "Starving people in, uh, India, and places like that." He amazed himself that he could concoct a suitable lie that quickly.

"Our freezer didn't break . . . ," Jessica began to protest, but Jack ushered her along before the nurse could follow up.

"Thank you," he said to her. "You saved my eyesight and you look young and slender in your nurse uniform. Nurses are so important."

She smiled and rubbed his head. Adults are always knocked off balance by compliments.

"You be careful, now," she said. "No more sticks."

The nurse looked at the paperwork again, and then at the jar of lollipops. "I better report this," she said, but then caught sight of her ample figure in the mirror and smiled.

"He's right. I do look slender," she whispered. "And young, too."

She helped herself to a lollipop and set down the clipboard, forgetting entirely any idea she had about reporting the incident.

CHAPTER TWENTY-ONE

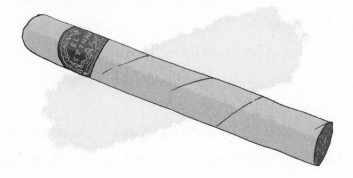

Mike's mom had come over that morning to join Jack's mom for coffee. Jack mumbled a good-bye to them, ran outside, and crossed the street.

He walked up to Mike's front door just as Mike came out to meet him. Mike had his basketball as usual, and an unlit cigar between his teeth.

"Is that real?" Jack asked.

"Yeah. I got it from my mom. I told her that cigars are so full of vitamins and minerals that I would never want one. Next thing you know, she's stuffing this in my mouth. That book is great."

"You're actually going to smoke it?"

Mike put it in his pocket and spit into the bushes. "Ugh!

Tastes terrible. Heck no. Those things will kill ya. I just wanted to see if I could get one."

He dribbled his basketball loudly on the sidewalk.

A black car pulled up at the end of the driveway and rolled down the window. Two men who looked like Secret Service agents were in the front seat.

"Hey, boys. Is that the Hartfield residence? Jack Hartfield live there?" the agent shouted, pointing with his thumb across the street to Jack's house.

The house number had been knocked off their house several weeks ago when Mike was trying to demonstrate a tricky way to spin a basketball on his foot.

"We don't talk to weirdo strangers," Mike yelled, backing up the driveway and pulling Jack with him. "But the Hartfields moved about two weeks ago anyway. Now they're over in the blue house on Edmonds Street a few blocks north. What are you guys, anyway, like a pair of weirdos out on weirdo patrol?"

Jack couldn't help but snicker.

"This is official police work, son," the agent said, and rolled the window back up. As they drove away, Mike ran a little closer to the street to get a look at the license plate.

"That WAS a government license plate," he said. "I wonder what your dad did. Maybe he cheated on his taxes."

Jack said, "You know that there's no Edmonds Street around here, right?"

Mike laughed. "Good one, huh? Those weirdos will be looking for that street forever!"

A look of concern flashed across Jack's face. Those were not regular police.

"Go get the book," he said. "I think I should go get Maggie."

"The book? What do you need the book for . . . ," Mike said, his voice trailing off as he watched another black car roll into the Wallaces' driveway next to Jack's house. A man dressed in a black suit stepped out and then another got out of the backseat, followed by Mr. Wallace.

"Hey. Those guys with Mr. Wallace look just like those other weirdos. What's he doing with them?" Mike asked.

Jack whispered urgently, "Go get the book."

"I don't have the book. I thought you had it," Mike said as he continued to bounce the basketball in front of him.

"Maggie must have it," Jack said, his face full of worry.

"So let's go get her," Mike said, and took a step in her direction before Jack stopped him.

Jack was watching the men across the street. He waved at Mr. Wallace, and Mr. Wallace waved back feebly. He looked tired, and much, much older than he had looked just a couple weeks ago.

One of the men was Agent Washington. He put his hand on his hip as he talked on his cell phone. He suddenly swiveled his head and looked directly at the boys.

"You know who he's talking to, right?" Jack whispered. "He's talking to the weirdos in the first car—the ones you sent to Edmonds Street. They probably just told him that you sent him on a wild-goose chase."

"Sent who on a wild-goose chase?" Maggie asked, and both boys jumped.

"Maggie! Don't sneak up on us like that!" Jack gasped. He looked down at her backpack, which she was swinging carelessly.

"That the book in there?" he said quietly.

"Of course it is," she said happily. "Why are you two acting so weird?"

Mike's basketball suddenly jumped out of his hands and wobbled on the driveway. Mike stared at it, confused, and Jack and Maggie looked as well, trying to figure out what Mike was staring at.

It was smoking. There was a peculiar electric smell in the air, like when a motor runs too long. And small crackles of blue static flickered for a moment around the ball.

The electric blast had come from Agent Washington's immobilizer. His abduction experience was still fresh in his mind, and he wasn't going to take any chances.

Before Maggie could say anything, she was whisked along with Jack and Mike. Years of Nerf battles taught them to NOT THINK, JUST RUN. They ran alongside Mike's garage and into his backyard. In a blink they were over the fence and in the yard of the people behind Mike's house.

"Those guys were shooting at us! With some kind of electric thing," she screeched, and they both shushed her.

They climbed the fence one house over to the left, and then started circling back again in the direction of their own street, staying low behind the hedges.

"We're headed right back toward them!" she whispered, trying her best to keep up. She really didn't want to follow them, but it was clear that they had done this sort of thing before.

"They won't expect this," Jack said. "They'll think we kept on going in the direction they saw us leave."

In spite of her fear, Maggie smiled at the plan. *Turns out boys are pretty sneaky, too*, she thought.

They crouched down in the bushes and listened quietly. Dogs were barking in the yards behind them. They knew that meant the men had pursued them over the fences and were looking for them on the street behind them now, exactly as Jack and Mike had predicted.

"They said they were police," Mike said.

"Real police do *not* usually shoot at kids," Maggie said. "This is about the book. It must be. I mean, look what we've been able to do with it."

"They'll go to our parents next," Jack said. "Let's just give the book back."

"I have to pee," Mike said.

"He has to pee when he hides," Jack explained.

"I don't think we can just give the book back," Maggie said. "These guys shot at us before they were even sure we had it. They are not the type of people that are going to just pat us on the head and let us go."

Jack nodded. "She's right. We can't stay here, though. Eventually they'll figure out we doubled back, and Mike will probably wet his pants."

"It's happened before," Mike said solemnly.

They stood up and peered into Mike's backyard and saw no sign of the agents. They quietly slipped over the fence into Mike's yard, and snuck along one side of his house.

"My bedroom window is unlocked. You know, in case of burglars. If a burglar gets in, I don't want a locked window to slow me down if I have to escape," he explained to Maggie.

Maggie looked at him with disbelief.

"Mike. An unlocked window is exactly how a burglar would enter your house in the first place," she said.

Mike stopped in his tracks and thought about it for a minute. "Yeah. Okay, I'm never going to leave this unlocked again."

He opened the window quietly and pulled himself in. "You're smart, Maggie," he added.

Jack and Maggie climbed in after him and surveyed his room. The walls were covered with posters of video games and basketball. Candy wrappers and socks and empty fast food bags covered the floor.

"My mom's over at Jack's house. C'mon. Get my mom's car keys," Mike told them. "We have to hurry before they get back. But first I have to pee."

"Car keys?" Maggie looked at Jack for some sort of reassurance.

"It's fine," he said. "We'll be fine."

Mike came out of the bathroom, and Maggie handed him the keys, her hand brushing against his.

"Why aren't your hands wet?" she asked.

"Cause I didn't pee on them," he said.

"But you washed them, right?"

"Why would I wash them if I didn't pee on them?" Mike said, and they hurried to the garage.

"Look," Maggie began, "I'm having a hard time believing that you *didn't* pee on them, but even if you didn't, people wash their hands when they use the bathroom, Mike."

Mike stopped and turned around to face Maggie. He grinned and put on an old hat that belonged to his grandpa.

"People *used* to wash their hands, babe. Before we got the book. People *used* to wash a lot of things."

CHAPTER TWENTY-TWO

Mike peered out the tiny window of the garage.

"I don't see any of them out there," he whispered. "Let's go."

He got into the driver's seat, put on his safety belt, pressed the garage door opener, started the car, and pulled slowly out into the street. Maggie and Jack were slumped down in their seats.

"Nice look," Jack said.

In addition to his grandpa's old hat, Mike was wearing sunglasses and had a cigar clenched between his teeth.

"This is so I'll look like an adult," he said, and he drove carefully around the corner.

Maggie, in the backseat, peeked over the top of the seat. She watched as her house disappeared from her view.

"Stop. Stop the car," she said, her voice panicky and urgent.

Mike stopped. "Why? What's wrong?"

"We can't do this. Mike isn't old enough to drive. We can't run off like this without telling our parents where we are."

"She's right," Jack said. "We can't do this. We'll just tell our parents what happened. There's an explanation. They'll fix it."

Mike spit out the cigar.

"Guys, I am so glad you said that. I was thinking the exact same thing, but I didn't want to be the first one to wuss out. Thanks for wussing first, Maggie," he said sincerely.

Mike looked down at the car's dashboard. He was puzzled.

"Sorry, but I'll have to drive all the way around the block. I don't know how to go in reverse."

Mike turned the corner and was passed by one of the agent's cars going the other way.

"That was them. That was them. Do you think they recognized us?" Jack asked.

"Are you kidding?" Mike laughed. "This is exactly why I put on this disguise. So we wouldn't get recognized."

The agent's car squealed around and jumped on the gas. It roared up behind them, and one of the agents hung out the passenger window.

The immobilizer crackled and four blasts crashed into the trunk of the car. They felt the static in the air and smelled the car's burnt paint.

One charge shattered the side mirror and another cracked the back window.

Mike stomped the accelerator and the car surged forward.

"I think they recognized you!" Jack yelled, and Mike wrenched the steering wheel, forcing the car to whip around the corner and slam his passengers against the doors.

"You're going to get us killed!" Maggie screamed from the backseat as electrical blasts continued to hammer the car.

"He won't," Jack said. "Mike rocks at driving games. If anything, the faster we go, the better he'll do! It's just like a video game!"

The agents could hardly keep up. In Mike's mind, this looked exactly like a video game, complete with a timer and a score. He was a fantastic high-speed driver, and he swerved masterfully in and around traffic and managed to keep the agents from getting a clear shot. With each maneuver, he increased the distance between them, and soon led them by several blocks.

"I'm winning!" he shouted as he slammed on the brakes and crashed into a Federal Express truck.

"Oh, man! The games never have a parked truck on the road!" he complained, trying to restart the car. He turned the key again and again but it wouldn't start up.

"Game over!" Mike yelled. "That's it. We gotta run! Oh, man, I think I may have eaten some of that cigar."

Just then, a red minivan, going the opposite direction, stopped next to their car. The door slid open and a pretty girl with short, dark hair poking from under a baseball cap extended her hand.

"Jack Hartfield?" she said with a smile. "I'm Resistance. We're here to protect you. Climb in."

"We're not going with you," Maggie objected. "We don't know you."

"Maggie!" Jack urged. "You're right. We shouldn't go with strangers. It's wrong. But the other guys are shooting at us."

Maggie was terrified.

"I don't know, Jack. Mike, what do you think?"

She looked at the driver's seat and it was empty. Mike was already in the van.

She reluctantly unclicked her seat belt and the two of them jumped into the minivan. It drove down the street, safely concealing them from the agents, who, running toward Mike's crashed car, didn't even glance their way.

"You said your name is Resistance?" Jack said.

"I'm *with* the resistance. My name is Marion," she said.

The driver looked back at them and nodded a *hello*.

"That's Mole. He's an adult, but don't worry. He's not a parent," she said.

"How'd you know where we were?" Mike asked. "How did you know Jack's name?"

"We monitor the Parents Agency's transmissions."

"Parents Agency?"

"Yeah. That's who was shooting at you. They're well organized, but always a little behind us on technology. You know how parents are."

They all nodded.

"The Parents Agency believes that you may have seen a copy of the *Secret Parent's Handbook*. Some of them think you may even have a copy that was issued to . . ." She pulled out a small notebook and read from it, ". . . a Mr. and Mrs. Wallace. Your old next-door neighbors?"

"Yeah. Those were my neighbors," Jack said, uncomfortable that Marion seemed to know so much about him.

"So, do you have it?" she said with a grin, and Jack felt there was something dangerous in her dark eyes that didn't match the smile.

Jack and Mike traded looks and Maggie picked up on it.

"I only saw it for a minute," Jack said. "They put it out in their garbage. I found it while I was trash picking. I flipped through it, but it didn't really look like anything I wanted, so I left it there."

"But you should have seen this awesome drill he got. You plug it in, pull the trigger, and VOOSH, you get totally electrocuted," Mike said, and Jack nodded enthusiastically.

Maggie was impressed at how believably Jack lied and how automatically Mike supported it. She couldn't help but smile to herself.

"That's too bad," Marion said. "We really could have used it."

Mole pounded his fist on the steering wheel.

"We're going to take you back to headquarters," Marion

continued, "and see what you can tell us. We've been piecing together bits and scraps of this thing for years, based on fleeting glimpses, memories, and so on. Whatever you can recall will help."

Marion looked at Maggie. "I don't suppose *you've* ever seen a copy, have you?"

Maggie thought it sounded a little bit like an accusation.

"Copy of what?" she asked, and pulled her backpack containing the *Secret Parent's Handbook* closer to her side.

CHAPTER TWENTY-THREE

The minivan pulled into a parking lot of an old school that looked as though it had been closed for a long time. They drove up to a large garage door and honked the horn. After a moment, the door opened and they drove in, the door closing behind them quickly.

They followed Marion out of the garage and were watched closely by serious-looking kids of all ages in the hallways.

As they passed the school's old classrooms, they could see some were filled with boxes of supplies; others were outfitted like dormitories, with beds and dressers and TVs.

"You live here?" Jack asked.

"I don't, but a few kids do," Marion said. "For most of us, it's just a base of operations."

They walked into the gym, which had been converted into a large technological center. Dozens of kids manned computer monitors flickering with data and surveillance feeds.

"Looks like you guys operate a few websites," Maggie said.

Marion smiled. "Hundreds. It's the main way we fund our operation."

"Yeah. Exactly what IS your operation anyway?" Jack asked.

A very little boy with blond hair stood up from a chair and walked toward them. Marion saluted him and cast a critical eye at Jack, Mike, and Maggie.

"Salute!" Marion barked. "Salute the General."

Maggie and Mike saluted.

"The General?" Jack said with a cruel laugh. "What are you, like seven years old?"

"I'm General Dobson," he said. "I'm in charge of the Resistance here. And I'm NOT seven," he added indignantly. "Try seven and three-quarters."

"Yeah, Marion told us this is the Resistance," Mike said, putting himself in between Jack and the General. "What is it you're resisting—potty training?"

Mike laughed loudly, but only for a second. The General swiftly had Mike's wrist in a crippling judo hold that drove Mike painfully to his knees and had him squealing for mercy.

"We know you've seen the *Handbook*," the General said, releasing Mike's wrist.

"You do, huh?" Jack said.

"We do. We monitor the parents' transmissions. We'd like to find out what you saw, and how we can fit it in with what we already know. We're not the enemy here."

"Who, exactly, is the enemy?" Maggie asked.

The General clenched his teeth and scowled. "You know who the enemy is. The parents are the enemy."

The General walked over to a keyboard and activated a large monitor hanging on the wall. As he spoke, he clicked through the images.

"Parents," he began, "have been in charge since the beginning."

A picture of Fred and Wilma Flintstone holding Pebbles came on the screen.

He leaned over to one of the technicians and whispered, "Get a better picture of cavemen, will you?"

He returned to his presentation.

"What chance do kids have? What chance have we ever

had? They have *all* the candy, *all* the money, *all* the power. And they make certain that we can't get any of it."

Other kids in the control center nodded.

"They deny us our simple pleasures and make us endure algebra, brussels sprouts, and room cleaning, even though they *know* that none of these things will ever make us happy. Ever."

Marion raised her hand.

"Yes, Marion?" the General said.

"Also don't forget they make us, like, look both ways when we cross the street and not talk to strangers, like we're idiots," she said, trying to be helpful.

The General smiled. He looked at Jack, a bit embarrassed for Marion.

"Yes. Well. Thank you for that, Marion," he said gently, as though he was speaking to a much younger child.

An image of a plain-looking book came on the screen.

"And they have a *book*," the General said, which started a low round of booing among the Resistance members. He put up his hands to make them stop.

"It's a book of special information. We know it's called the *Secret Parent's Handbook* and we know that they take extraordinary measures to protect it."

The screen displayed a photo of one of the immobilizers used by the agents.

"I took that immobilizer off an agent myself," Marion said proudly. "It's *my* immobilizer."

"We're confident that this book is full of things they don't want us to know. It's full of things we could use to overthrow them and take our rightful place as the leaders of the world. They're not the boss of us."

The entire group of Resistance members shouted back in unison, "THEY'RE NOT THE BOSS OF US."

The General looked up at them with his fierce blue eyes.

"The Resistance has been around for decades, assembling a copy of the *Secret Parent's Handbook*—just like the one you saw."

"How much of it do you have?" Jack asked.

The General tapped the keyboard and brought up images of their cherished fragments.

"Quite a lot," he said. "Here's an eighth of page eleven, found in the remains of a house fire. And here's nearly half of page thirty-five, retrieved after it passed through a wiener dog. Here's a picture of me retrieving it."

The screen showed a photograph of the General, dressed in black, suspended by ropes lowered through a hole in a roof. It was a selfie of him smiling at the camera, holding up the scrap of paper as a wiener dog slept peacefully in the background.

Marion beamed. "The General is just the best at special retrievals."

Jack and Maggie and Mike nodded politely and tried to look impressed.

The General continued his official briefing. "Other little shreds here and there have turned up and our best minds have been laboring to reconstruct a complete book."

He swelled up with pride.

"Some of our scientists read at, like, a twelfth-grade level, you know."

"Yeah, this is great," Mike said. "Looks like you'll have this complete by the time you're—what—a hundred years old?" Then he chortled and snorted loudly, right in the General's face.

Marion shoved Mike hard and knocked him to the ground. She would have jumped on top of him, but the General stopped her.

"That's not the way it will happen, Mike," he said, offering him a hand up. "One day, a kid is going to find a complete copy or a nearly complete copy. Maybe it will be at a garage sale, or forgotten in an attic—something like that. You had a complete copy in your hand for a moment yourself, didn't you, Jack?"

Jack nodded weakly.

"And when that kid finds it—and hangs on to it—we'll be there. We'll read it, study it, and use the secrets of the book to finally put the parents in their proper place. We'll take over."

"You push like a girl," Mike said to Marion, still a bit embarrassed that she had knocked him down.

"I can do better," she said with a cruel smile, and shook a fist at him. "Wanna see?"

The General continued, "We're working with the few scraps we have in the meantime, to at least begin to make some small progress against the enemy."

"Or," Marion began. "Or if this plan doesn't work, we'll begin taking prisoners. We'll kidnap some parents, toss them into cages, and we'll question them until we get the answers we want."

Maggie winced.

"You think you can capture adults so easy?" Mike scoffed.

"We've already run a series of test captures, Tubby. It's

easy. When an adult hears a kid in trouble, they run right into our ambushes. It's a lot simpler than you think," she said with a cruel little giggle. A few of the other Resistance members laughed along with her.

"Kidnapping? Imprisonment?" Mike said. "Isn't that, like, majorly illegal? Not to mention that if a person thinks they are being kidnapped, they might do anything to fight back—somebody could get killed."

The General frowned.

"Marion knows that we are not kidnapping and questioning parents," he said.

"*At the moment*," she added quietly.

"Currently, we believe we can accomplish our goals without that level of violence. We WILL take over, friends, make no mistake. But for now, the position of the Resistance is that we will not take orders from parents without pouting, sulking, or throwing a fit. And when they want us to eat our vegetables, or wash our hair, or not put our feet up on the couch, we will demand an explanation!"

The Resistance members applauded.

Maggie clapped politely and said, "I know what you mean about parents, but actually, those three examples—vegetables, washing your hair, and keeping your feet off the couch—those things seem pretty easy to explain . . ."

The room went silent. She felt their eyes glaring at her angrily, especially Marion's. Mike nudged her. Jack shot her a look.

She got the message.

"It's, uh, because they're stupid," she said. "Parents are stupid. And everything they say is stupid. Stupid, stupid, stupid."

The General eyed her critically for a moment. And then he smiled.

A huge round of cheers and applause went up and the General beamed at her. "You'll fit in here nicely. Let me show you your rooms."

CHAPTER TWENTY-FOUR

Jack's mom hung up the phone. She had been speaking with Mike's dad.

"They don't know where the boys are either. Maggie's mom called a while ago and she can't find Maggie."

Jack's dad looked out the window. He did his best to sound upbeat.

"It's really not even that late. Lots of times we don't have dinner until seven, and Jack knows that. They're just running around somewhere, I'll bet. They'll show up any minute. You'll see."

Jack's mom hugged him tight. "I know," she said, her voice cracking slightly. "But . . . I just worry. I worry all the time. About everything. Since the day he was born."

"I know. I know. Me too. Let's have a look at the

Handbook. It will have something about how we should punish him so he doesn't do it again," his dad said.

"I really don't want—"

"I know. But we have to," he said, and he took their copy of the *Secret Parent's Handbook* from its secret hiding place, behind a stack of their old math textbooks from high school. "Let's see, getting home late . . ."

Just then, there was a knock on the door and Jack's dad jumped up to answer it.

It was Maggie's dad.

"Have you heard from them?" Jack's dad asked hopefully.

"No, but I think we're going to have to clear this book thing up. Mind if we come in?"

"We?" Jack's dad asked.

CHAPTER TWENTY-FIVE

Jack, Maggie, and Mike sat on some little beds in one of the Resistance dorm rooms.

"This should be okay, don't you think?" the General asked them.

"I'm not staying here," Mike said. "This is a dump. I'm going home."

"They're looking for you, Mike," the General said. "Your home isn't really your home at the moment. That book, the *Handbook*, is *everything* to them. It's how they control us. Whatever secrets it possesses are essential to them and their power. For some reason, they think you have a copy, or think you've seen enough of it that you are a threat."

"So, when they find out that they're wrong, they'll leave us alone," Jack said.

The General laughed bitterly.

"When was the last time you heard an adult admit they were wrong about something? They still wear clothes that are ten years old because they won't even admit they've gone out of style."

Maggie giggled in agreement. "I know! My mom has this one horrible dress that she can barely even fit over her wide a—"

The General interrupted her.

"No. All you can hope for now is that they believe you really *do* have a copy, and maybe we can use that belief to negotiate for your freedom."

Marion added, "Remember, they *shot* at you."

"That thing probably just stuns you," Mike said. "Besides, I'm like a ninja. I'll get into my house without them even seeing me. Without them even smelling me. I'm a smell-ninja. That's a ninja that even dogs can't detect."

He punctuated the statement with a threatening karate pose directed squarely at Marion.

Marion raised an eyebrow at Mike's plump physique and cast a doubtful look at Jack and Maggie.

"Tell you what. Let's hear what you remember from the book; then we'll talk about where we go next from here," the General suggested.

"I was the only one who saw it," Jack said quickly. "These two have nothing to tell you."

Maggie was touched by his protectiveness.

"Then tell us what you saw," the General said.

"I only glanced at it, you know. It just looked like some dumb old book. It was supposed to look like a collection of turnip recipes."

"Yes, turnip recipes. Of course. I see. Go on."

"I remember a couple chapter headings like 'Face-Making' and 'Not Finishing Dinner.' But I don't remember anything other than that. I didn't read any of the strategies."

"Interesting that you would refer to them as 'strategies' if you didn't read them," the General said with some obvious distrust.

Maggie suddenly spoke loudly, almost yelling.

"Oh my gosh. Oh my gosh. Oh my gosh!" Her voice was filled with urgency. She waved her hands wildly.

Jack and Mike were confused by Maggie's sudden outburst.

"My parents have a copy! I've seen it. It's labeled *Turnip Recipes*. We never have turnips, but I've seen them looking through it a jillion times. I know exactly where they keep it. We won't have to wait a hundred years for this, will we, General?"

She touched his arm and he stared down at her hand.

"I, um," the General stammered.

Suddenly her mood changed. She seemed sad. "But you guys are right. Those agents are looking for us. There's probably no way to get past them. I mean, you'd have to be a genius . . ."

She smiled at the General and he blinked several times before awkwardly smiling back.

CHAPTER TWENTY-SIX

Agent Washington and other agents sat in a black car in front of Jack's house. They were trading information on their cell phones as a little boy crept up behind their car and stuck a device underneath their bumper.

Agent Washington spotted him in the rearview mirror.

"Hey, kid! What are you doing back there?"

"My ball rolled under your car. I'm trying to get it."

"Get out of here. You could break your neck that way."

The boy walked away and secretly spoke to somebody on his cell phone.

Moments later, the red minivan that the kids had escaped in with Marion pulled up slowly in front of Mike's house, and the agents slid down in their seats and quietly watched it.

"It's them," Washington whispered into his phone, and he reached for his immobilizer. "The three targets are back, as predicted."

The minivan door slid open and the three kids climbed out slowly with their heads down.

Suddenly, Washington threw open his car door and yelled, "FREEZE!" He began firing immobilizer blasts in their direction.

The kids jumped back into the minivan and it took off squealing, throwing dirt and dust as it sped around the corner.

"All units! All units!" an agent yelled as their shiny black cars took off in pursuit of the minivan, the agents inside shouting into their microphones and activating their immobilizers.

They raced through the turn, squealing tires and raising a cloud of dust and exhaust.

After they were completely out of sight, a small blue car rolled up slowly with Marion behind the wheel. Jack, Mike, and Maggie climbed out and looked around.

They were all wearing different clothes now—the decoys in the red minivan the agents were currently chasing were wearing their original outfits.

Jack laughed. "How long before they find out that those kids in the minivan aren't us?"

"The Resistance is clearing traffic ahead of them all the way to the next state. That minivan has an extra gas tank, and Mole is the best driver I've ever known. Plus, we planted a magnetic pulse detonator on the agency car that will go off in a few minutes and disable their communications and their blasters. They won't be able to shoot at the van, and they won't be able to radio for backup. They'll have no choice but to keep following them. My guess is that it will take them at least eight or nine hours to figure out that those kids are fakes."

"So, uh, we'll call you when we have the book," Jack said.

"The second you have it, press the CALL button on the phone we gave you. It's programmed with our number, and we can track you with the GPS in the phone. As soon as we get the signal, we'll be there to extract the book."

"And us," Maggie said. "You'll extract the book and *us*."

Marion nodded. "Right. The book and you."

As the three began to walk away, Marion motioned Maggie back over to the car.

She smiled sweetly and Maggie leaned in a little to hear her.

"You better get that book, little girl," Marion said. Her voice fell to a threatening, low whisper. "The General won't be able to keep me from kidnapping indefinitely. Lots of the other Resistance members agree that abducting and interrogating parents is a much easier way to accomplish our goals."

"Why are you telling me this?" Maggie asked.

"I wanted you to know that I'm planning on grabbing your parents first. Then Jack's, then Plus Size's over there."

"I'm getting the book just like you asked," Maggie said, her voice trembling.

Marion leaned in close and whispered to Maggie.

"Your family will be the first I put in cages if you don't bring us that book," she said as she pulled away.

Maggie swallowed hard and ran quickly back to her friends. Mike was eyeing his house worriedly.

"We're late," Jack said. "I'm in trouble."

"*You're* in trouble? I stole the car and wrecked it," Mike said. "Will you guys walk in with me so I have somebody to back up my story?"

"We're all in trouble," Maggie said. "I believe what the General said about this book. It's more important to the parents than we realized. And I don't know about you guys, but I think letting the Resistance have it might be as bad as what the parents do with it. Maybe worse."

"You don't *really* know where your parents have a copy, do you?" Jack said to Maggie.

"Of course not. But we had to get out of there. What else could I say?"

"See, she *destroyed* the conversation, Jack," Mike said. "Just like your ol' pal El Destroyo. We're a good team, Maggie. We should destroy something together sometime."

They followed Mike into his house.

"I think you could be right. I think the General would probably abuse the power," Jack said.

"Like we did," Maggie said quietly. "But way worse. It makes me so mad that our parents have been manipulating us, but we did it right back as soon as we had the chance. Can you imagine how Marion would use it?"

Jack cringed.

"Mom! Dad! I'm home!" Mike yelled.

Nobody answered.

Jack's eyes fell on a huge scorch mark on the wall, and

then another. They followed the path of burnt spots to the bathroom door, which had been smashed in.

"Mike . . . ," Jack began.

"They took my parents?" Mike said in disbelief. "They took my parents?" he repeated, finally yelling, "they took my parents!"

"Oh my gosh," Maggie said. "They probably took all of our parents."

The three ran to Maggie's house. The lights were on, the front door was open, and the couch was still warm from an immobilizer blast. Her parents and brother were gone, and the same scene awaited them when they searched Jack's house.

Tears streamed down Maggie's face, and Mike was working hard to hold his back.

"We have to call the police," Maggie said.

"You're right, Maggie," Jack said. "This has gone way too far."

"Jack?" Mike said, rubbing his eyes. "You don't think they'll come back here to find us, do you?"

"Nah," Jack said. "They're busy chasing the decoys. They have no idea we're even—"

A blast of energy tore past them and slammed into the wall, sending sparks flying.

The smoke briefly concealed them and they darted out the back door and scrambled over a fence.

They ran for blocks and blocks, one of Mike's arms flapping helplessly behind him.

They finally had to stop to catch their breath, and they hid in some bushes. They crouched there, panicked, wheezing, frightened, and without a plan.

"I think they grazed me. They got my arm. It feels like it's asleep. I can't move it."

"We should have called the police," Maggie said.

"And what?" Jack yelled. "And what? And get hauled off to wherever it is they took our parents?"

"I have to pee," Mike said.

"You can't," Jack said. "If you stand up, they might see you. Just hold it."

"I can't, dude. I'm going over into those other bushes. I'll ninja pee so nobody can see me. Besides, we lost them anyway," he whispered, and quickly shuffled off.

The two sat there quietly, waiting for Mike to return.

Finally, Maggie whispered, "You know, it just occurred to me that we didn't double back like you taught me before. We ran in a straight line."

Jack nodded. "Yeah, we probably should have been a little more—"

In a neighboring bush, Mike crouched down. "I can't get my zipper open with one hand. Jack, will you come and help me get my zipper ope—"

An immobilizer flashed and crackled and Mike fell face-first into the bush between them.

"Mike?" Jack said, shaking his friend gently.

There was another blast and Maggie fell over on her face with a thud.

Once more the immobilizer struck, and Jack felt an intensely painful stinging sensation surge through his entire body. Everything went dark as he fell forward and heard the sounds of the agents talking on their cell phones.

CHAPTER TWENTY-SEVEN

Jack felt a hand on his cheek.

"Jack. Wake up, sweetheart." The soft, gentle voice made him feel good.

"Mom?" Jack whispered.

"No, I'm a nurse. But your mom is here, sweetheart. Do you want to talk to her? You have to wake up, Jack."

Jack opened his eyes. He was in a small room with a white-haired nurse sitting in a chair next to his bed.

"What happened?" he said.

The nurse looked over toward the door. One of the agents was standing there, staring intently at Jack. The memories suddenly came back to him.

He sat up quickly. "Where's Maggie and Mike?" he demanded. He swiveled his legs around to jump out of the bed, only to find that one wrist was handcuffed to it. "Take this off me!" he shouted. "Right now!" He rattled and tugged at the handcuffs.

The agent walked over and removed an immobilizer from the holster under his jacket. He waved it threateningly at Jack.

"Baby need a pacifier?" he asked Jack with an ugly smile.

Jack looked at the immobilizer and calmed down.

"You said my mom was here. I want to talk to my mom."

"Oh, we'll all talk pretty soon," the agent said, and returned to his position in front of the door.

Jack thought for a moment. He thought about the *Handbook*.

"Yes," Jack said. "You're right. We *should* talk. I think we should talk about personal responsibility. I think we should talk about doing the right thing. What do you two gentlemen think that means . . . ?"

The agent and the nurse smiled and sat down on the bed next to Jack as Maggie was dealing with her own problems a few hallways over.

"You can't keep me here!" Maggie shouted angrily. "You can't just shock people and drag them off and lock them up!"

An agent stood in front of Maggie's door, and a man in

a suit was sitting on the edge of her bed, watching her try to get his handcuff off.

"Those are neat handcuffs, aren't they?" he said. He was official, but friendly. He reminded Maggie of a school principal.

"No. Well, yes, they're a little bit neat. But you can't lock me up like this. Are you the police? The government? Unlock these."

"I'm Mr. McMaster," he said with a bright smile. "But a lot of the people here just call me the Supervisor. That's a funny name, huh? It's like a spy name."

"You're a spy?" Maggie said, clearly not believing him.

"Not a spy—not exactly. Look, let's go talk to your parents about the book and stuff like that. You like gummy worms? I'll get you gummy worms if you promise not to give us any trouble."

Maggie looked over at the agent. "He'll blast me with that weapon of his if I don't do what you say, right?"

The Supervisor laughed. "Yeah. You'll be asleep before you hit the ground."

"Okay. I won't give you any trouble. Keep your worms. Where are we going?"

"Let's go to the Family Room," the Supervisor said, unlocking her handcuffs.

They walked down several long hallways, escorted by two agents. The Supervisor kept a fatherly hand on her shoulder.

A technician stopped them and put a clipboard in front of the Supervisor. He read it for a moment and turned to Maggie.

"Green, yellow, or blue, Maggie; which color gumball would you pick?" he asked her with a smile.

"Are you serious? *Blue*," she grumbled. "Of course."

"Make them blue," the Supervisor said happily to the technician, and signed the document on the clipboard.

They continued walking and he patted Maggie's shoulder. "We're running tests on some special medicine we can hide in gum and candy to make kids, uh, *behave better*," he said. "I probably would have chosen green. Thanks for your help."

"You're *drugging* kids?" she asked, horrified.

"Well, not yet, Maggie. But I'll let you in on a little secret: We will be soon. You and your friends are actually helping me convince others that it's necessary. I want to start drugging them right away," he said with his broad, friendly smile.

"Why? Why would you want to do that?"

"Maggie, kids today are smarter, much smarter than they used to be. And they're so great at technology. Eventually, I'm not sure we'll be able to control them with the simple strategies in the *Handbook*, and we'll need to just—you know—slow them down a little."

"When are you going to do this?"

"Oh, I don't know for sure, Mags, not exactly. See, not everybody here *completely* agrees with me on this one. But it will happen soon. Sooner than some people think."

After what seemed like a mile of busy hallways, they arrived at their destination.

The Family Room, as he had called it, was a huge space filled with gigantic screens and computers. Countless men and women were monitoring videos and data coming in from what looked like all parts of the world, and it reminded Maggie of a very expensive version of what the Resistance had set up in the old school gym.

Technicians scurried around on catwalks, in a hurry to share their information with other technicians.

The armed agents moved around more slowly. They

watched the monitors and talked in whispers to each other. Maggie could feel them staring at her.

She and the Supervisor began walking up a staircase to a large door, guarded by the biggest, toughest agents Maggie had seen so far.

"Wait," Maggie said. "Aren't you worried that I'll tell people what you're doing? That this whole big scheme of yours will be discovered?"

The Supervisor stooped down so that he was eye to eye with Maggie. His smile faded.

"Since you asked, Maggie, my dear: No, I'm not worried about *you* telling people anything."

The doors opened wide into an enormous conference room, three walls of which were covered with monitors. The fourth wall was a large darkened window that looked down on a street. Maggie thought she recognized the area but couldn't tell exactly where they were.

Jack's parents were there in the room, sitting next to Jen and Mike's dad. Maggie's parents stood up when they saw her.

"MAGGIE!" her mom called out, and a pair of agents quickly made certain they stayed seated.

"Are you okay, Maggie?" her dad said, and her mom started crying.

"I'm fine. Where's Sean?" she asked. Then, noticing Jack's little sister wasn't there, she said, "And where's Jessica?"

The Supervisor smiled and directed Maggie to a seat next to her mother.

"You see that?" the Supervisor said. "Your Maggie is looking out for the youngest ones. You can't teach that. She has the instincts," he said. "She'll make a terrific little mommy one day."

Maggie was annoyed at the Supervisor's praise. "Where are they?" she demanded.

Jack's dad said, "They're at a Chuck E. Cheese's with Mike's mom. They think it's one of their friends' birthdays. They're okay."

"But we saw the scorch marks on the wall. Didn't they abduct you all?"

"We convinced the kids that it was a game," he said. "The *Handbook* is pretty good at stuff like that."

The door opened and Agent Washington, along with two others, brought in Mike. He was handcuffed, his feet were chained, and they had some sort of gag locked over his mouth. He was fighting them every inch of the way.

"Where's Jack?" Maggie asked.

"Oh, he'll be along," the Supervisor said, chuckling. "He's pretty clever, that Jack. He used some stuff from the book and actually talked his way out of his cell. Can you believe it? He persuaded the guard and nurse to set him free. That book is pretty powerful stuff."

The Supervisor pressed a few buttons and looked up at a monitor that was playing a recording from security cameras. There was no sound, but they saw Jack walking down the hallways, explaining something to the guard and nurse, who were nodding in agreement and following behind him like puppies.

The Supervisor snickered and took a long drink of coffee. His voice was suddenly a bit less jolly. "Well, you kids know that already."

"He'll get away," Maggie said with a defiant smile. "You'll never catch him."

The door opened and two agents walked in with Jack and guided him to a chair.

"It's powerful stuff," the Supervisor said, "but it's really only effective when you don't know it's being used on you. Once you know what somebody is doing, it doesn't work very well. The nurse and guard weren't prepared for Jack to break out a strategy on them. More experienced guards caught him at the front exit."

Mike started mumbling something from underneath his gag, and his dad spoke up.

"Can't you take that thing off him?"

"Maybe," one of the agents said angrily to Mike. "Are you going to be a good boy if we release you?"

Mike nodded. "Okay," he said, his voice muffled underneath the gag.

"And NO biting," Agent Washington added, his face decorated with three Band-Aids.

"Those were ninja-karate-face-bites," Mike said as they removed his gag and the rest of his restraints.

They escorted him to a seat next to his parents, and his dad hugged him so hard he couldn't breathe.

The Supervisor took a seat at one end of the table, and a door opened slowly behind the large seat at the other end of the table.

"I'd like you all to meet the head of our operation, Big Mother," he said.

CHAPTER TWENTY-EIGHT

Big Mother closed the door behind her and looked around the room. She wasn't very old, or big, and Jack thought there was something very familiar about her.

"Hello, everyone," she said. Her voice was soft and friendly. "Quite an adventure we've had, don't you think?"

The door opened and Mr. Wallace walked in, escorted by an agent.

"Ah. Mr. Wallace. Mostly your fault we're even here today, isn't it?" she said, irritated.

"Yes, but I did help recover it. I did clean up after myself, Big Mother."

Big Mother bowed her head and closed her eyes, repeating the phrase almost like a prayer. "Clean Up After Yourself."

The agents and the Supervisor quietly whispered it as well. "Clean Up After Yourself," they chanted softly.

"Yes, Mr. Wallace, you did. And you're very lucky that Mr. Dooley here reported the suspicious behavior. It could have been worse if it had gone on longer."

Maggie's head spun around to confront her dad.

"YOU reported us? Dad? YOU did this?"

His eyes filled with tears.

"Maggie, I had no idea that this is how they handled things. They tell us to report stuff, for your safety. You have to believe me, Mags, I didn't know."

"Maggie, sweetheart," Big Mother said to her, "if it makes you feel any better, we picked up the first piece of information in a phone call that we intercepted placed by Mr. Wallace. Your dad just confirmed it."

Maggie did feel a little better.

"Because we've contained the leak, you won't be punished, Mr. Wallace," Big Mother said in a tone resembling a judge's. "This agent will take you downstairs to fill out the paperwork and then you can go. Florida, right? Maybe I could visit you sometime?"

"I'd like that," he said, thinking how much he wouldn't like that. "Thank you, Big Mother."

The agent escorted Mr. Wallace out. As the door closed, Big Mother pressed a button on her intercom.

"Mr. Wallace won't be leaving the building," she said. "Please have him shipped to a correctional retirement facility in the morning."

Big Mother turned her big blue eyes toward Jack and Maggie and Mike.

"And you three rascals . . . ," she said with a little laugh and a playful wag of her finger. "You three scamps read the *Handbook*, didn't you?"

Mike had been punished enough times to know where this was going. He put his hands on the edge of the table and pushed back, ever so slightly. Behind him, he heard two agents activate their immobilizers. His escape plan was not going to be possible.

Big Mother stood up. The meeting, as far as she was concerned, was over.

"You three will be going to a reprogramming facility in Antarctica, where we will try to erase your memory of the book and its contents. You could be out in as little as four years."

"Where do you get the authority?" Maggie's mom demanded.

Big Mother took a sip from her coffee. "Mrs. Dooley, the Parents Agency has been around for a very long time. We're in many countries, and we have representation in most branches of the government. The Supervisor and I were recognized for our outstanding abilities as parents and were appointed to the positions we now hold. So we don't actually need to 'get' the authority from anybody. We *are* the authority."

The Supervisor cleared his throat.

"Getting back on track here. It takes more like five years to reprogram the old way," the Supervisor said. "But maybe only three if we use the medicine."

"Three to five years, then," Big Mother said, dismissively waving her hand. "We'll work it out of your little heads as quickly as we can, and you'll remain there until we no longer view you as a threat to the operation."

"They're just kids!" Maggie's dad exploded. "Why? Why do they have to go to your . . . prison?"

"Because I said so," Big Mother said, and the others in the room bowed their heads and repeated it back.

"Because She Said So," they chanted softly.

"Could you please—" Maggie began. "Could you please return my backpack? I have to give my parents their car keys."

"Such a sweet girl," Big Mother said. "Certainly. I thought you might be looking for it." She handed the backpack to Maggie.

Maggie smiled and clutched at the bag.

"We took the *Handbook* out, of course, dear. I replaced it with a few books I enjoyed when I was your age. You'll have a lot of time for reading, you know."

Maggie's face fell.

Jack asked, "Will we be able to talk to our parents while we're in prison?" He turned and looked directly into Maggie's eyes. "Like, will we be able to *phone*?"

She suddenly got what he was trying to communicate with his stare, and she smiled.

Under the table, she felt around inside her backpack. They had left everything else in it, including the phone the Resistance had given her. She held down the SEND key and smiled back at Jack.

"Or can we *send* them letters?" Maggie said, letting Jack know she had picked up on what he was saying.

"There has to be some sort of appeal process," Maggie's dad said. "They didn't know what they had. They're not going to tell anybody anything."

Big Mother stared flatly at him. "It's only a matter of

time before the Resistance finds out about this. Then they'll come looking for them, and that's when things could get really messy. The Resistance is a powerful force to be reckoned with, I assure you. Unless you want to see Sean and Jessica and Jen thrown in prison for good measure, I suggest you shut your mouth and don't talk back to me."

The agents lowered their heads. "Don't Talk Back to Her," they whispered.

"Wait a second! I'm an adult," Jen shouted. "And I'm about to be a parent myself."

"You're going to have a baby?" Mike said, his eyes bulging.

"I would have liked to tell you differently," she said. "But yeah, I'm going to be a mom."

"You aren't one yet, missy," the Supervisor said through his permanent smile. "And until you are, you don't have any rights here."

"Well, we're done here now, I think," Big Mother said. "This was a very positive talk. You kids have fun in prison and be good."

As she prepared to walk out, five masked members of the Resistance, decked out in SWAT gear, swung through the window of the conference room with a huge crash. Glass flew everywhere as the kids and parents dove under the table. Agents fired immobilizers wildly, striking four of the Resistance fighters and sending them hard to the ground.

"Where's the book? Where's the book?" Maggie recognized Marion's voice shouting from behind her mask.

Mike's dad leapt over the table and twisted an immobilizer away from an agent. With flawless marksmanship he fired around the room, putting a single charge squarely into the chest of every guard in the room.

"Whoa! Where did you learn to shoot like that?" Mike said.

"I've always been a pretty good shot, Mike."

"Not when we play video games. Your aim sucks."

"I, uh, kinda go easy on you, Mike," he said, and threw an arm around him.

Jack and Maggie quickly locked both doors to the conference room. Jack grabbed one of the unconscious agents' weapons. He pointed it at the Supervisor.

"You're going to let us walk out of here," he said.

"Not without the book," Marion added, removing her mask. "Where's the book?"

Jack jammed the immobilizer right up in the neck of the Supervisor.

"Yeah. The book. Give us back our book and get out of the way," Jack said roughly.

The Supervisor looked at the small light on the handle of the immobilizer and smiled. "Jack, there are hundreds of agents behind these doors—what are you going to do, hold them all off with the single charge left in that immobilizer?"

"We won't have to. We're going to hold them off with the *Handbook*," Maggie said.

"You don't have the *Handbook* anymore, cupcake," he said. "Remember? We took it out of your backpack."

Maggie pulled a small flash drive from a pocket in her backpack and held it up. "Who needs it?" She smiled smugly. "I scanned the whole thing onto this."

Marion jumped nimbly to the windowsill and grabbed a rope still dangling from where they had crashed through the window.

"Throw it here!" she yelled, preparing to make the catch and swing to freedom on the street below.

The Supervisor lunged for Maggie, and Jack fired the

only charge in the immobilizer and missed. Maggie's dad leapt and tackled the Supervisor in midair.

Mike grabbed the flash drive from Maggie's hand. He had been practicing shooting baskets in his driveway since he was five, and he knew he could make this shot. He cocked his arm back, threw the flash drive, and watched as it flew through the air, bounced off the ceiling, a wall, another wall, and then onto the table directly in front of Big Mother.

"I thought I could make that," he said.

Marion sat down on the window ledge and groaned.

Big Mother picked it up and looked at it. "The whole book is on here? Amazing. You know, maybe *we* should do it this high-techy way. We could do it this way, couldn't we, Supervisor?"

"Well, yes, probably. But we're actually a little behind schedule in certain kinds of technology. You know, it's a shame we can't just hire kids for our computer stuff. They're so good at it."

"Give it back," Jack said.

"No worries," Maggie said.

Big Mother quickly removed her shoe and brought the

heel down hard on the flash drive, breaking it into several large bits.

"There. That's that," Big Mother said sweetly.

"I could still recover data from that," Maggie said calmly.

Big Mother's eyes glared and she brought her heel down a dozen more times on the broken flash drive bits.

And then a dozen more.

And then a dozen more.

She smiled at Maggie; she was wheezing a bit and sweating.

"I could still get data off that," Maggie said calmly.

Big Mother angrily scooped up the bits and dumped them into her coffee. She stirred it violently with a spoon and sneered at Maggie.

"Still could," Maggie said confidently.

Big Mother exploded. "OH, YOU COULD NOT!" she bellowed. "And that's that. So now let's put down the little immobilizers and get on with things. You kids need to pack."

"You think that was my only copy?" Maggie sneered.

A look of concern flashed across Big Mother's face. The Supervisor's smile collapsed.

"Maggie, dear, even if it wasn't, we'll merely pick up your computer from your house, and then we'll have your other copy, won't we?"

"You know how the Internet works, right?" Maggie said with a small, insulting snort.

"Yes. Of course I do," Big Mother said uncomfortably. "I have done web surfing." Her voice became angry. "I bought this blouse from the online."

Mike laughed as he repeated it. *"From the online."*

Big Mother shouted, "Adults invented the Internets! Don't you forget that!"

Maggie folded her arms and locked eyes with Big Mother.

"There are copies in places that will be posted at a certain time tomorrow, and the day after that, and the day after that. Automatically."

"Rubbish. You don't know how to do that."

Maggie's dad sighed. "She *does* know how to do that. I've seen her do it."

Big Mother's face turned red.

The intercom buzzed and a nurse's voice came on. "I'm told that people were blasted in there. I should have a look at them. Can I come in?"

The Supervisor explained:

"When people get hit with one of these charges, it's important that we make sure they're okay. Some people can have a dangerous reaction. The effects are temporary, but if somebody gets hit too many times, they can be out for days, maybe even a week. It can be bad. In some cases, it could kill somebody. Please. Let her come in and at least have a look at the kids."

"Okay," Jack said. "No tricks." He waggled the immobilizer at him. "I could still hit you with this thing."

Marion dropped a couple immobilizers on the floor.

"About all you could do. These are all empty."

The nurse came in and started looking over the Resistance SWAT squad. One at a time, she went about the business of taking pulses, lifting their masks, and checking their eyes.

The Supervisor sat down hard in his chair.

"Kids. There's something you need to know, about why the *Handbook* must remain a secret."

"No," Big Mother said quietly.

"We're at a standoff here, Big Mother. We have to do *something*."

"No," she repeated quietly.

As the Supervisor looked across the table, he realized that Big Mother hadn't been responding to what he was saying at all. She was looking at one of the Resistance squad. The nurse had just removed the General's mask.

"Billy?" she said, her voice a gasping whisper. "Billy is part of the Resistance?"

"He's the General," Marion said. "He's the *leader* of the Resistance. How do you know him?"

Big Mother's wide, frightened eyes had filled with tears. "He's my son," she whispered.

CHAPTER TWENTY-NINE

The nurse administered shots to revive the General and the others who had been hit. They wobbled slightly as they stood up and groggily rubbed their eyes.

"So," Jack said, "what's it going to be, Big Mother? The *Handbook* posts tomorrow online, unless, of course, you're ready to bundle up your little Billy there—since he knows about the book, and that means he's coming with us to Antarctica, right?"

Big Mother's eyes fluttered, and a tear spilled down her cheek. She stared at the Supervisor, hoping he had an answer for her.

"Don't ask me," he said. "I wanted to start using medicine to subdue them, like, ten years ago."

Big Mother sighed deeply and looked into Maggie's eyes. Then she looked at her son.

"Supervisor, please tell security to stand down," she said.

"Mom?" he asked with disbelief. "You're part of the Parents Agency?"

"I am, Billy. I just . . . I don't know what to say right now."

"Is this the headquarters?" he asked meekly.

"It is, son," she said.

The General looked around the room and purposefully locked eyes intensely with Maggie.

His eyes darted over to Marion's backpack lying on the ground. He nodded slightly.

CHAPTER THIRTY

The small group walked around the headquarters, and the Supervisor issued orders to them as they passed.

"This location has been compromised, people. Prepare to move to a new secure location. No fingerprints, folks. Clean it up. We're out of here in a week."

Big Mother gave her son—the General—a big hug.

"So you're the head of the Resistance," she said, her voiced filled with mixed feelings of shame, anger, and pride. "We've been after you and your group for quite some time. You've really been a thorn in our paw."

The General pulled away from her angrily.

"Why do you do this? Why do you have this terrible *Handbook*, these stupid, mean rules? Why do you work so hard to keep us beneath you?"

"Keep you beneath us?" the Supervisor scoffed, and Big Mother put up her hand to quiet him.

"Okay. You want answers," she said. "I understand that. You all have been at this a very long time. We can give you some answers."

Jack narrowed his eyes and said, "Yeah. Tell us everything, but do NOT try to use one of the strategies on us. We know how those work."

"Let me start," the Supervisor said. "Let me show you the Archives. Maybe you'll agree with what we're doing. Maybe you'll decide not to post that file, Maggie."

He gave her a friendly, practiced wink and she sneered at him.

"Your tricks won't work on me, you know," she said.

He put his hands up as if to surrender.

They all walked into a large set of rooms off the main control center. There were displays behind glass and on pedestals. It resembled a small museum.

The Supervisor led them to a case with an old, thin, tattered scroll inside it.

"The *Handbook* is old, *very* old. This is the first version we know of. It dates back centuries," he said.

The General rapped on the case and smirked.

"Of course, over time, things have been added, and translated," the Supervisor said, "but the main stuff is unchanged. And, of course, everybody went to great efforts to keep the material hidden from children."

They looked into another case with various copies of the *Handbook*. Each had a false cover with a title no kid would ever pick up, like *New Ways to Wash Behind Your Ears*, *The Pilgrims Loved Algebra*, and *So You Want to Sweep Out the Garage*.

As they walked, they saw a display of mannequins depicting a young family. The mom was holding a baby, and the dad was holding a copy of the *Secret Parent's Handbook*. Both were smiling down at their child.

"A copy of the *Handbook* is given to all parents when they have children. It's to help them . . ." The Supervisor paused as he searched his mind for a word that wouldn't offend his listeners. ". . . to help them *raise* their children."

Marion clenched her fists. "More like *control* them," she muttered with disgust.

"Well, yes, to a certain degree, to control them," Big Mother said. "But that's not all."

"Kids are complicated. They're difficult," the Supervisor said, gesturing slightly in the direction of the General.

"They're always trying to poke their eyes out or break their necks."

Big Mother bent down to speak directly to the General. "Which reminds me, Billy, no more swinging on ropes through plate-glass windows. You could break your neck."

Maggie squeezed her mom's hand tight enough for it to hurt. "You shouldn't lie to us. Why do you tell kids lies, like that if they make a face, it could freeze that way?" she demanded.

Big Mother looked at the Supervisor and he shrugged his shoulders. They looked around at the other parents for an answer.

They all shrugged.

"I don't know," she finally admitted. "That's what the book says we should tell you. I guess it just bugs us when you make those faces."

The Supervisor said, "You see, kids, parents have a relatively short amount of time with you as children. Most of your life will be spent as an adult. A very small percentage of it will be as a child. So we have to launch you straight, like little rockets, in the right direction. The book helps us do that."

"Yeah, but if you don't know *why* the book says things—like how you had no idea about making faces—how do you know that us little rockets are going the right way?" Jack asked.

"Yeah," Maggie added. "And all these little 'rockets' are different. Maybe they don't all want to head in the same direction."

Jen rubbed her stomach.

"It's going to be . . . so hard," she said. "I mean, my baby isn't even born yet, but I can tell . . . I can tell what's going to happen."

Big Mother put her arm around Jen's waist and pulled her close.

"Tell them what's going to happen," Big Mother said softly.

"I'm going to love this baby so much that it's going to *own* me," Jen said with a sweet smile.

The Supervisor nodded. "It's true," he said. "The book isn't to hold you kids *down*. You kids own us the minute you're born, even before. The book is to help *us* get up to *your* level."

Big Mother said, "You may find it hard to believe, but we love you *so* much that we're practically powerless against you. We think about you every minute. We're crazy about you no matter what you do. When you ask for candy for dinner, we *want* to give it to you, just to see you smile.

When you want to jump off the garage roof to see if you can fly, we want to let you, because deep inside, we believe that maybe you really can."

"Without that book, we parents would probably put every child on earth in the hospital in a week," the Supervisor said. "Or worse."

"That's all very nice, but look how it's worked out," Marion said, pulling herself up to her full height. "You give us answers like 'Because I said so' and you make us learn stuff we'll never, ever use. You say that you do all this because you love us, but really—what difference does it make if we make our beds or not? We're going to be sleeping in them again that night."

Big Mother looked to the Supervisor for the answer to that one. He shrugged.

"No idea," he said. "It's kind of a fair question."

Marion clenched her teeth and shook her fist. "Why are we even going through this? When that book hits the Internet, and every kid on earth knows what it says, you know what will happen?"

"The kids will control the parents." Mike grinned.

"That's right. THE KIDS WILL CONTROL THE PARENTS. We'll do whatever we want, whenever we want. Then you can see how you like being bossed around for a change."

Big Mother flopped down in a chair.

"We *already* saw, Marion. We were kids once, too," she sighed. "And we got all the same rules, and reasons, and punishments you get, and we hated them as much as you do. But eventually, when we became parents ourselves, we changed. Kids are the most complicated, most important, most difficult things in the world, and they don't come with a manual. Over time, parents began to feel that the stuff in the book is, well, it's probably better than nothing."

"It's not," Marion said. "It's not better. And none of that matters now anyway."

"Easy, Marion," the General said softly.

"Maggie has the material out there. Tomorrow it posts. Freedom for kids begins tomorrow," Marion said triumphantly. "We WIN."

Mike applauded and cheered.

Big Mother cast a defeated look at the Supervisor, and he hung his head.

Maggie looked at the parents. She didn't see anything like anger. She saw worry—pure, undisguised worry, and Jack saw it, too.

They knew this wasn't right.

"I guess I could stop that from happening, if there was a good reason to stop it," Maggie said quietly.

Marion glowered at her.

Jack grinned. He understood where she was going with this.

"I don't know, Maggie," Jack said. "I mean, the problem here is that we all love each other. And it's impossible to turn *that* into something good."

Big Mother and the Supervisor smiled. Jack was using a strategy from the book:

> The child loves to prove you are wrong, and takes delight in contradicting you. When you want to make a point, state the opposite, and the child, like a fish, will take the bait and argue.

"Wait a second," the General said, getting tangled up in their strategy. "Loving each other *is* a good thing. You're wrong, Jack. It's not a problem."

"Stop it!" Marion shouted. "They're tricking you, General. That file is going to post tomorrow and we will finally get our way. All the time. About everything."

"Look, Marion," Maggie said angrily. "*You* don't get to tell *me* what to do. I can stop that post anytime I want, if I feel like it."

The General had seen that terrible anger in Marion's eyes before, and he lunged for the display of mannequins, snatching the copy of the *Secret Parent's Handbook* from the mannequin dad's plastic hand.

"Not if you're asleep for a week, you can't," Marion said to Maggie, and she pulled out an immobilizer that she had smuggled out of the conference room. She gritted her teeth and fired every charge in it at Maggie.

Maggie cowered, and the General leapt with the book outstretched, the blasts intended for Maggie striking the book with sizzling impacts.

Marion lowered her immobilizer slowly as the General stood up.

"Why? Why did you stop me?" she asked. "You . . . you betrayed me."

"I'm just not sure anymore," he said, shaking his paralyzed hand. "I used to be sure and I'm not sure now. I think this battle is changing, Marion. I mean: Look at these adults; we're going to *be* them someday, and then we'll be on the other side of this."

Marion looked at the parents, and then looked at Jen. It suddenly occurred to Marion that Jen wasn't really that much older than she was.

Mike laughed and slapped the General on the back.

"Whoa! Nice leap! I thought you were such a little punk and then you went all James Bond and Han Solo and stuff. Like if Batman and Spider-Man had a baby, and it was really, really supershort, like maybe malnourished and sick, and bad at sports, that would be *you*!"

"Billy," Big Mother began. "I mean, General—I'm glad you understand why we must continue to use the *Handbook*." She smiled hopefully.

"It's not up to him," Maggie said abruptly. "*I'm* the one with the file. And we *are* making changes around here, Big Mother. That book of yours, this whole organization, the secrets, the lies, it has to change."

Big Mother stood and stared at her angrily. "And just why is that, young lady?" she said.

"Because I said so," Maggie responded.

Jack pointed at Maggie proudly.

"She's in charge," he said.

CHAPTER THIRTY-ONE

For two whole hours, there was a lot of explaining.

Big Mother told the kids what the parents had been doing, and the General told everybody what they had been attempting as well.

"I can't believe you called my parents," Marion said sourly.

Marion's mom stroked her hair and Marion pulled back, away from her touch.

"Marion," her mom said, "we never meant for you to feel controlled."

"But all the rules all the time," she said. "They're so stupid."

Her dad looked at her through his glasses. He was tall and strict, and spoke very little.

He cleared his throat and said, "Marion. Maybe some of

the rules are stupid. But we could just never stand the idea of you . . . you know . . ."

"What, Dad, growing up?" she said, annoyed.

"Being hurt," he said, and her angry eyes softened.

"We don't always know what to do, Marion," he said, his deep voice cracking. "We just—we love you, little girl. More than anything in the world. You are everything to us."

Her mom spoke softly. "You never knew your aunt Marion, sweetheart. You were named after her, you know. She was your dad's little sister. I never knew her either. She passed away when she was just a child, and your dad has missed her every day of his life. He always felt that she hadn't been protected very well. He can't help protecting you so, Marion. I can't either."

Her dad spoke carefully, trying to control his cracking voice.

"But I can do better, Marion," he promised.

"I've said that exact thing," Marion said quietly. "I've said that exact thing so many times."

He put out his arms toward her.

"Maybe . . . I'll let you try to prove it," she said softly.

She had been angry for so long that she could hardly remember the last time she felt like a little girl, but she allowed herself to slowly lean into her dad and be swallowed up by his giant hug.

The General could not believe it was really Marion.

"Ewww," said Mike, witnessing the hug.

Jack said, "Look, we get the rules, at least some of them." And he talked about what they had learned over the past couple of weeks, and that he had come to believe that maybe parents weren't always the enemy. You actually can get sick of eating candy all the time.

Mike shook his head in disagreement.

"Speak for yourself," he said, patting his ample gut. "You just don't know how to commit yourself to it. You really should have tried the gummy bear soup I invented."

Jack ignored him and went on to say that they had realized they would probably grow up into lazy, stinky dummies, adding that Mike had stopped washing his hands after he went to the bathroom long ago.

The adults thrust bottles of hand sanitizer at Mike.

"Okay," Maggie said, "I admit we need rules. But why do you need so many? Why does there have to be a whole book full of them? Parents can come up with their own rules, and be flexible enough to change them sometimes."

Big Mother smiled.

"I would have never believed that kids would arrive at the conclusion that they really needed certain rules. I wonder if maybe we've been . . . underestimating you. I'm delighted to see that you understand why we can't just eliminate the Parents Agency, or get rid of the *Secret Parent's Handbook*."

"I don't understand," Mike said, and the whole group fell quiet. "I'm not going along with this. You do have to eliminate it."

"Mike, think it through," Big Mother said sternly.

"That, Big Mother, is exactly how I DON'T like to think things: *through*."

A few of the agents began to reach slowly for their immobilizers.

"Let me tell you how I see things," Mike began.

The Supervisor put a hand on Maggie's dad's shoulder. He leaned in and spoke in a whisper.

"While Mike there is speaking his mind, let's talk in private, just for a moment. Bring your wife and Maggie. This will just take a second."

Jack looked back over his shoulder and watched as Maggie and her parents walked into the conference room and closed the door behind them.

CHAPTER THIRTY-TWO

"Look," the Supervisor said to them, "I was afraid that this whole negotiation was going to go bad. Have a peek at this." He pulled a check made out to Maggie from his pocket and handed it to her dad.

The Supervisor spoke quietly and quickly. "How about if we just *buy* the file from you, Maggie? We'll still—you know—improve on this whole handbook business. But there's not enough time to make this happen right now. Everybody feels too rushed. The deal is falling apart out there. Any moment, we might get impatient, or the Resistance will get impatient, and somebody is going to do something hasty. When the smoke clears, who knows who will be in Antarctica?"

Maggie glowered at him.

"Wha—, wha—," her dad huffed in disbelief, his eyes wide, as he examined the amount of the check. "That's a lot of money. A LOT of money."

Maggie's mom said, "And if we take this deal you're proposing, none of the kids will be punished? Nobody gets in trouble?"

The Supervisor smiled and nodded. "It's a better solution, isn't it? You guys can buy a new house, heck, a few new houses. You can retire. The kids go to college, get new cars. All that stuff. And dolls. Think of all the dolls! You like dolls, right, Maggie?"

Maggie smiled and plucked the check from her dad's hand. "Oh, I just love 'em," she said. "Can I have a minute to talk about this with my parents?"

"Of course," the Supervisor said with a big warm smile, and left them alone in the conference room.

CHAPTER THIRTY-THREE

The Supervisor nodded confidently at Big Mother.

Mike was just wrapping up his speech.

"And that's why, no matter what your parents think, you *should* be able to eat a chili dog while you go to the bathroom," he concluded.

"Where's Maggie?" Jack asked the Supervisor.

"She'll be along shortly, I'm sure," he said, thumping Jack playfully in the shoulder.

"I want to talk to her," Jack said, and the Supervisor smugly leaned against a wall and winked at him, then flashed a thumbs-up to Big Mother.

"Thank you for your valuable input on chili dogs, Mike," she said. "I think we're done here," and she nodded at the security staff.

"Yes," the Supervisor said. "Let's all just go have a little rest."

The security agents took ahold of Jack and Mike and their parents as well. They unholstered freshly charged immobilizers.

Mike's sister, Jen, was also being hustled along by the agents, when Maggie's dad emerged from the conference room.

"So," he said, "I think it's probably a great idea if we all run as fast as we can out of this building."

"And why's that?" Big Mother demanded.

"Because Maggie set the bombs that Marion brought with her in her backpack."

The General looked at Marion and smiled.

"I'd be surprised if they don't take out the entire block," he said.

CHAPTER THIRTY-FOUR

Maggie held the rope as her mom clumsily slid down from the conference room to the sidewalk below. The Parents Agency had never been attacked before and the defensive security was a little sloppy. They hadn't boarded up the window the Resistance had smashed through, or removed their ropes.

"So happy they missed this," Maggie said, wagging Marion's backpack as she and her mom ran to their car.

"Are you sure about this, Maggie?" her mom said. "I mean, setting bombs. Honestly, I don't even like you to light the scented candles at home."

"Just drive, Mom. I'll tell you exactly where to go."

Inside the Agency, alarms were going off. The security officers were running around in a panic.

"Go in there and disarm those bombs this instant, young man," Big Mother barked at the General.

"Disarm them?" he scoffed. "I can't even get near them. Once they're armed, the slightest touch will set them off."

"I suppose that was your idea?" Big Mother said to the General. "Not a very good idea, young man."

"That was *my* idea," Marion said. "The General added a remote control that you could use to shut them down safely from a distance."

Big Mother's face brightened.

"WONDERFUL! Where is it?"

"I destroyed it," Marion said. "And THAT was my idea, too."

Mike, Jen, and their dad pushed past them.

"Hurry up!" they shouted.

"Yeah. We only have a few minutes to get out of here," Maggie's dad said, and threw a handful of shredded paper at the Supervisor as he ran past.

It was the check he had given to Maggie.

"She's too old for dolls," he said, and then looked back and chuckled. "You probably should have known that. Kids. What are ya gonna do?"

The Supervisor looked at the bits of paper blowing around on the ground.

"I thought they liked them until they were fourteen or something," he said. "I have sons."

The tires on the minivan squealed.

Maggie's mom cranked hard on the wheel as Maggie gave her directions.

"Turn here. Go all the way down to the light and turn left."

She opened the backpack and pulled out a detonator that looked exactly like the one she'd set at the Parents Agency.

"Dear," her mom asked gently, "is that safe?"

"It's safe, like, for *a bomb*, Mom. A bomb is kind of like the *opposite of safe*, wouldn't you say? They aren't very useful if they're safe."

A black minivan roared up behind them. Maggie spun around to see agents raising their immobilizers.

"We have company, Mom."

People streamed out of the Parents Agency, running for their lives.

Pretty soon, when they were safe a few blocks away, Jack and Mike stopped and looked back at the building.

Big Mother and the Supervisor were staring back at it; they seemed utterly brokenhearted.

Mike walked up to them and touched them lightly on their backs.

"I guess things happen for a reason," he said gently. Big Mother ran her fingers through Mike's hair and smiled through her tears at him.

"And the reason here is because you suck."

Just then a series of dull, thudding pulses echoed out of the headquarters.

Their hair blew back slightly and they felt a low vibration in their chests.

"Was that the bomb?" Big Mother asked.

Maggie's mom's car screeched to a stop and they jumped out and ran into the Resistance hideout.

Electrical charges fired by the agents crackled past them as the agents pursued them inside.

Maggie pressed buttons on the detonator as they ran down the hallways to the main control room. She locked the door to keep the pursuing agents out.

"Okay, everybody," she shouted. "Run for your lives!"

The kids spun around and stared at her.

"You know what this is." She held the bomb aloft. "This is one of Marion's."

She set it down in front of the main terminal and pressed the button to start the countdown.

"It's over!" she barked. "Everybody out!"

The kids just looked at her, unimpressed.

"That's not a bomb," one of the kids said. "That's a magnetic pulse detonator. It will take out the computers, but it won't hurt us."

Maggie walked calmly over to a fire alarm.

"Yeah, but you know how much trouble you'll be in for a fake fire alarm?" she said, and she pulled the handle.

The alarms blared loudly. The kids remained seated.

Maggie was at a loss.

Her mom inhaled deeply.

"EVERYBODY OUT!" her mom screeched, and the kids all stumbled to their feet and ran out the doors, just as the agents were running in.

"IT'S A BOMB, YOU FOOLS!" she hollered at the agents, and they turned and tripped out after the kids.

Maggie looked at her, amazed.

"Yelling is kind of a built-in mom thing. You can't learn it from a book."

As they drove away from the evacuated hideout, they heard the sirens of the fire engines approaching. The dull thudding pulse of the detonator fired and they could feel the vibration from it.

"That will mess up their computers," Maggie said. "And when the firefighters get there, they'll clear out all the stuff that's in their headquarters."

"Did the detonators destroy everything the Parents Agency had?" her mom asked.

"No way," Maggie said. "It caused problems for them, but I'm sure they had backups on everything."

CHAPTER THIRTY-FIVE

Sean and Jessica played Whac-A-Mole as the racket of the Chuck E. Cheese's clattered around them. Their families, along with Mike, Marion, and their parents, sat crowded around a table with Big Mother, the Supervisor, and the General. They smiled as kids ran past with armloads of tickets and smears of birthday cake across their faces.

"How long until all the parents destroy their copies of the books?" Jack asked.

"Well, Jack," Big Mother began, "it will take some time. We'll send out the instructions, just as we agreed, but that magnetic pulse of Maggie's wiped out a lot of our data, and at present, nobody is sure where we put the backup stuff to contact everybody."

The Supervisor shrugged sheepishly.

"Kids are better at computer stuff," he said. "I've said that all along. We should have hired some."

"So this will all take a while," she continued. "But we'll keep at it. I promise."

The Supervisor pointed his finger at the General and Marion.

"And that Resistance of yours, you're disbanding that, right?"

"As long as you stick to the agreement," the General said through a mouthful of pizza.

Big Mother grinned and resisted the urge to tell him not to speak with his mouth full. Instead, she turned and wagged her finger playfully at Marion and spoke to her parents.

"This girl of yours is a real firecracker," Big Mother said. "If she can focus that intensity of hers, there's nothing she won't be able to do."

"It's hard to believe that just a few hours ago we were enemies," Marion said, reaching into her jacket. She pulled out an immobilizer and Big Mother froze.

"I guess I should give this back," Marion said, putting it on the table with a heavy thunk. "I kind of took it."

Big Mother quickly snatched it off the table and hid it in her purse.

"We weren't enemies," she said. "Enemies hate each other. Our conflict came from wanting to *control* each other, and that's different from hate. If we all agree to just control *ourselves*, then maybe we can reduce some conflict. Do you agree?"

The General thought for a moment.

"If everybody agrees to that," he said, "then I think this can work."

Jack's mom said, "You're going to let Mr. Wallace go, right?"

"Yes, of course. I was wrong to have him shipped off," Big Mother said. "I can see that we actually have a lot of things we'll have to go back and have another look at."

Jack's eyes popped open wide. "Did you just say you were *wrong*?"

"Yes, Jack. Adults *can* do that."

For just a moment, Jack thought he had a glimpse of what Big Mother might have been like as a kid. He thought he probably would have liked her.

The Supervisor noticed the General talking to Maggie and Mike. He leaned and whispered to Jack.

"On the subject of having a look at things, you better have a look at the General over there. He's chatting up your girl."

"She's not my girl," he said as he spun around and trotted quickly in her direction.

"So, Maggie," the General said, discreetly standing on his tiptoes, "we should stay in touch. You know, like hang out. You can text me or whatever."

Mike interrupted the General as Jack walked up.

"That's not going to work for us," Mike said. "Maggie is Jack's girlfriend, and also a little bit my girlfriend because we found her together. So, no hard feelings or anything, but no—no, you can't have any contact with her for any reason ever. Unless you'd be willing to trade me for Marion. I'll trade my half of Maggie for Marion. She's a little gooshy now, but deep down, I think she's still a pretty good woman."

Maggie slugged Mike hard in the arm.

"I can talk to anybody I want to! Yes, you can call me, General."

"Great. But I guess I'm not the General anymore. I think I'm probably just plain old Billy now. Or Bill. It's Bill," he said, lowering his voice.

"Right. Bill. Text me sometime, Bill," Maggie said, and turned to Jack.

"Can you believe him?" she asked, jerking her thumb at Mike, who was already off with his dad to order another pizza.

Jack smiled. *"A little bit his girlfriend,"* he repeated. "I'm *so* sure."

Maggie's big green eyes twinkled.

"You're not even a little bit his girlfriend," Jack said, and he reached down and took her hand.

The two of them followed their families out of the Chuck E. Cheese's, stopping only long enough to wave good-bye and see Marion sharing a laugh with her parents.

Alone together by a Pac-Man machine, the Supervisor and Big Mother waved good-bye.

"So is this it?" he asked her.

She nodded.

"You know, we could always, you know, kind of . . . go back on the deal, for their own good," he said.

"No. This is the new reality. We have to settle for an uneasy peace. As long as we don't do anything, she won't post the book. As long as she doesn't post the book, we'll keep up our side of the bargain."

"What makes you so sure that they'll stick to it?" the Supervisor asked.

"A mother can tell," she said. "Maggie's a good girl. She's honest. We can count on her. Jack, too."

"What about Mike?"

"Oh, hell no," she laughed. "He's exactly like you when you were his age. But those other two can keep him in line."

The Supervisor patted her gently on the back.

"It seems a little too easy to me. They agree, we agree. These policies were in effect so long; why were they so easy to dissolve?" he asked.

"I was thinking the same thing. I think that sometimes wars end quickly because neither side really wanted to be at war in the first place. It's a huge relief just for it to be over."

"I guess you're right," he said with a long, tired sigh. "I really won't miss the job. It's no fun being the bad guy. And I can always go back to my old job where everybody loves me—as a substitute teacher."

"Eventually," she said. "But we saw what three basically good kids could do with the *Handbook*. Imagine what a bad kid could do with it. They could manipulate unprepared teachers, police, aunts, uncles."

The Supervisor watched a child take a piece of pizza

away from his crying sister and throw it into a Skee-Ball target.

"Every book has to be accounted for," she said. "Every last one of them has to be destroyed. Until we have them all safely back, we'll need to keep watching, but that's all we'll be doing: watching."

It was clear that she was emphasizing it in order to keep the Supervisor in line.

"Watching," he repeated back.

CHAPTER THIRTY-SIX

Sometimes summer days roll past like a dirty, under-inflated little beach ball, wobbling and wiggling, and then coming to a stop on its plastic nozzle, which somebody neglected to stuff up inside it.

Other times, they roll past like a thunderous roller coaster, clattering and shaking with screaming howls of laughter exploding from the wild-eyed riders.

And still other times, you're on that roller coaster, and agents from secret organizations are shooting at you while you try to preserve and protect society for the benefit of future generations of kids and parents, and somewhere near the end of the ride, you make all the other riders promise to try their hardest to make the ride better for one another, or you'll crash the roller coaster and that will be the end of the fun for everybody.

Jack and Maggie sat on Mike's lawn, tossing handfuls of grass at each other. They waved off mosquitoes and looked up at the darkening sky.

Mike and his dad were both trying in desperation to sink even a single basket as Maggie's mom and dad walked up and stopped on the sidewalk.

"Getting late, sweetheart," Maggie's mom said, resisting the impulse to brush Maggie's hair back from her face.

Jack's mom and dad and little sister, Jessica, waved from across the street.

"Hey," Mike said, "did Maggie tell you? My sister is going to have a girl, so I'm going to be an uncle."

"No—since it's a girl, you're going to be an aunt," Maggie said to him, and he stopped dribbling the basketball for a moment to think about it.

And he thought about it for a moment more.

"You're wrong, Maggie. I'll still be an uncle."

Maggie giggled. She stood up and brushed off her shirt.

"See ya, Jack," she said. "Bye, Aunt Mike."

Jack ran across the street to his house.

"Hey, I saw somebody looking at the Wallace house

today," he told his folks. "I hope they have a big dog for me to tease and then stick my fingers through the fence so it can bite them off."

His mom whirled around, about to shout at him, when Jack and his dad burst into laughter.

Maggie and her parents started walking slowly home. It was a beautiful summer evening, with crickets chirping and a gentle breeze playing through her wild hair.

Maggie's dad hugged her hard.

"It's been a couple weeks now, Maggie, and I've been meaning to ask you, exactly where did you learn how to upload a file so that it would automatically post at a certain time?"

"I can't do that," she said with a smile.

He stopped and stood and stared.

"So, back when they had us at the Parents Agency, with the immobilizers and the agents, and you were about to be sent to a prison in Antarctica, you were *lying*?" he asked, his eyes wide with astonishment. "You weren't *really* able to do that?"

"Nope. But you told them that you had seen me do it. You were lying, too."

"Let's call it bluffing," he said.

They laughed at each other.

"But I really *did* have a backup," she said. "I have the file saved on a flash drive that I have hidden in my room."

"Maggie, sweetheart, eventually they would have found that," he said.

"No way, Dad, it's hidden super-well. *Nobody* is that good at finding things."

Her dad smiled at her and turned to Maggie's mom.

"Hey, I know. Get Sean and let's go out for late-night ice cream. You want to?"

"Okay, great!" she said, and she poked her head in the door and called up to Maggie's little brother.

"Sean! You want to go out for ice cream?"

"Yeah! Give me one second," he called down to her from Maggie's bedroom, which had always been his favorite place to snoop around when left alone for a few minutes.

A mischievous smile curled on his lips at the flash drive in his hand, and he slipped it into his pocket for later inspection. He ran noisily down the stairs to join them.

"Here I come!" he shouted happily.

CAN'T GET ENOUGH OF JIM BENTON? CHECK OUT DEAR DUMB DIARY!

#1: Let's Pretend This Never Happened

#2: My Pants Are Haunted!

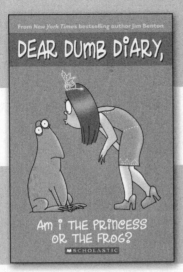

#3: Am I the Princess
or the Frog?

#4: Never Do Anything,
Ever

#5: Can Adults Become
Human?

#6: The Problem With Here Is
That It's Where I'm From

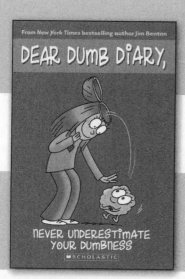

#7: Never Underestimate
Your Dumbness

#8: It's Not My Fault I Know
Everything

#9: That's What Friends
Aren't For

#10: The Worst Things in Life
Are Also Free

#11: Okay, So Maybe I Do
Have Superpowers

#12: Me! (Just Like You,
Only Better)

YEAR TWO #1: School. Hasn't
This Gone On Long Enough?

YEAR TWO #2: The Super-Nice
Are Super-Annoying

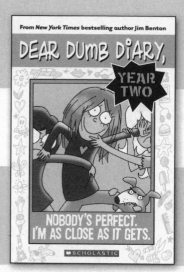

YEAR TWO #3: Nobody's Perfect.
I'm As Close As It Gets.

YEAR TWO #4: What I Don't
Know Might Hurt Me

YEAR TWO #5: You Can
Bet On That

YEAR TWO #6: Live Each Day
to the Dumbest

Dear Dumb Diary, Deluxe: Dumbness is a Dish Best Served Cold

WWW.SCHOLASTIC.COM/DEARDUMBDIARY

ABOUT JIM BENTON

Jim Benton is an award-winning author and artist. You may know some of the other things he's made, like It's Happy Bunny, Dear Dumb Diary, Franny K. Stein, Victor Shmud, and more. He's developed a TV series, written books, and produced a movie. He always did everything his parents told him to do. Pretty much.

Jim lives in Michigan with his wife and kids and can be found online at jimbenton.com.